KILLSTANBUL

A WORK OF FICTION

Matthew Di Paoli

MILFORD HOUSE

an imprint of Sunbury Press, Inc.

Mechanicsburg, PA USA

MILFORD
HOUSE

an imprint of Sunbury Press, Inc.
Mechanicsburg, PA USA

For information about special discounts for bulk purchases, please contact Sunbury Press Orders Dept. at (855) 338-8359 or orders@sunburypress.com.

To request one of our authors for speaking engagements or book signings, please contact Sunbury Press Publicity Dept. at publicity@sunburypress.com.

FIRST MILFORD HOUSE PRESS EDITION: May 2025

Set in Adobe Garamond Pro | Interior design by Crystal Devine | Cover by Lawrence Knorr / Cover image by Kevin Funkhouser | Edited by Anaiah Davis.

Publisher's Cataloging-in-Publication Data
Names: Di Paoli, Matthew, author.
Title: Killstanbul / Matthew Di Paoli.
Description: First trade paperback edition. | Mechanicsburg, PA : Milford House Press, 2025.
Summary: *Killstanbul* is a quirky, off-genre pulp crime novel(la) set in the winters of Reykjavík, Prague, and Istanbul. Carolus, an Icelandic native hitman, navigates a tangle of women, attackers, and ancient cities looking for the unfortunate mark he's paid to kill.
Identifiers: ISBN : 979-8-88819-264-1 (paperback).
Subjects: FICTION / Action & Adventure | FICTION / Humorous / Dark Humor | FICTION / Travel & Vacation.

Designed in the USA
0 1 1 2 3 5 8 13 21 34 55

For the Love of Books!

To Tori for believing in this book
and
To Christina for the OG edits

PROLOGUE

Carolus plunged his fork into the puffin, twisting it in its blueberry Brennivin sauce as his waitress approached the table. She had brown hair that ended abruptly at her round shoulders. Her dark mascara, lipstick, and fingernails rendered her paler than she already was. There is nothing paler than Iceland.

"Are you doing OK here? How about another?" Her thick lips moved with a Polish lilt.

"How can I say no?" Carolus wasn't on the job, and he rarely refused whiskey.

She leaned her sizeable breasts over his plate, an action too blatant to be an accident. Women know where their breasts are at all times, Carolus thought. They have mental lists of those allowed to glance at them, those allowed to see them, and the few allowed to grope them. They were hardly covered by her tight striped cotton top.

He always had a way of knowing when women wanted him. Carolus's mother had said once that "if he put half as much time into work as he did into girls, he'd be as respected as Yanni." It was somewhat of a dated reference, even then, but the effect was the same.

* * *

Out on the Laugavegur, compact sedans skittered over an ice patch. The same ice patch that manifested every year. It rained snow in the cold, uncommitted way Reykjavik turns all weather wet. Christmas lights faded in the mist down the lengthy street. To Carolus, it didn't seem like the holidays. The holidays of his youth were exuberant, sheltered from the frost like a summertime Eskimo.

The next time the waitress came to fill his wine glass, Carolus gently grabbed her collar and pulled her close. His index finger lingered in the warmth between her breasts.

"I want you to bring me dessert and then come to my apartment."

He slid a bronze key onto a napkin, writing the address to his apartment on the flimsy tissue paper.

He released her and she straightened up. Her chlorine eyes, her lips, her tartar sauce skirt enthralled him. He wished he could stick his whole face underneath and inhale. She probably smelled like frozen orange slices.

She stared, confused by his boldness. His messy black hair and second-day scruff added to his disheveled look. He hadn't landed a substantial job in a while and was working cheap just to drum up business. His sweater had a hole in the back that he hid with the chair.

"We have peach and cottage pie," she said, trying to gather herself.

"Peach," Carolus said.

She took the key and left.

* * *

That night, they lay in bed together. The red-walled modernist studio made him feel close to her. The floors were black and white checkerboard, and the kitchen could barely fit a dog. Four stainless steel spoons hung over the two-burner stove. A pot of SpaghettiOs grew a thin orange film. Carolus rarely used the fridge, so only a can of Red Bull, a bottle of expired ketchup, and seven bullets lay cooling inside. The bullets, of course, he kept in the butter hatch.

She stroked his hair and brought him between her breasts.

"You remind me of Icelandic class in compulsory school," Carolus said.

"A girl?"

"No." He slid his lips up to hers. "I like this spot right here. Don't you ever have the urge to build something?" He remembered an old Erector set his father got him for Christmas once. He built it up until it was over his head, and he imagined he would live at the top of it one day. Now all he did was tear things down.

"Like a website?"

He pointed to a spot just above her left cheek. "Maybe a small community. Very exclusive. It would have its own tennis club, and maybe right here you can own your own restaurant." He pointed to the tip of her nose. "No more waiting tables."

"Why is the restaurant on my nose?" She laughed.

She kissed him and got up, stood stinking naked in front of him—almost reflective from his sweat so he could make out his body in hers. Her breasts drooped a bit. She was beautiful. He noticed small bruises on her shins and her thighs. He wondered if he'd made them.

She turned and tiptoed on the cold wooden floor to the bathroom. The door didn't shut properly, so he could make out the line of her body through the slit. He rolled away from the shadow of sweat on the bedspread.

"How many men have fought for you?" he called out and buried his face in her perfumed pillow.

"Only two," she said from the bathroom, the water running, "but they were very small and no one was hurt." She said it as if she were disappointed.

His vocation provided its own types of battles. He recalled some of the more fantastic demises in his line of work—choking by goat hair in milk, the blow of a cricket ball. These were not acts of God. He'd learned a long time ago that God does not act quickly; a person must take it upon himself to carry out judgment. Not many are willing to do this.

The waitress returned and fit herself neatly into the cradle of Carolus's long body. "I will stay for one more hour," she said.

CHAPTER 1

December 11

Carolus walked to the bus depot at the edge of Reykjavik where German tourists gathered in search of the Northern Lights. Legend said the Northern Lights only showed themselves to those with hearts willing to forgive.

The tourists would not see them that night. Instead, they would wait in the cold, comforted insufficiently by their guide who told stories of woodland elves.

At the station, Carolus rented a Jetta and drove south. As soon as possible, he would need to steal clean plates. His mark lived in Grindavik, a town known for its mineralized waters and Viking culture. On the roadside, Carolus placed a blond wig on his head and secured it with bobby pins he'd taken from his sister's turquoise jewelry box. He replaced his dress shirt with a plain T-shirt, covering it with a fluffy black coat he'd picked up at a downtown thrift store. It smelled like maple syrup. He rolled a ski mask into a cap and wore it over his wig.

The countryside hung low against the steel railing of the highway. The black rock of eruptions, the blue moss—Carolus could feel the warm power of the water beneath him. It boiled beneath all of Iceland, thick and sulfuric, warming bathtubs and springs. He felt the vibration in his hands and gripped the wheel. The countryside loomed beautiful and disastrous. The land's green and cornflower merged from the rock, lighting the roadside.

Near the mark's house, Carolus found lodging at the Blue Lagoon Clinic and lay down twenty small bills, enough to cover his two-day arrangement.

He carried his leather bag up to his room and removed a DHL box harboring the following items:

1. Disposable silencer
2. Blue rubber gloves
3. Hollow point ammunition
4. Clean black tennis shoes
5. Disassembled fixed barrel Ruger Mark II
6. Manila envelope

In the bathroom, Carolus reviewed the contents of the envelope. He snapped on the gloves and assembled his weapon, wiped each part for fingerprints. Loaded the clips. Wiped the bullets. The man is stout, he told himself. He likes to take dips in the hot springs. He is a strong swimmer. Bald with three moles on his back. He is always shaven. His wife is not home from 0600 to 1800 hours. He works as a disc jockey—what kind of man works as a disc jockey?

With a disposable lighter, Carolus burned the envelope and client information. Later he would burst the lighter on a rock.

With his clothes on, he lay in bed and set the small red hotel clock to 0500 hours. The room glowed a soft shade of green, and Carolus wished for a drink. He was not to drink on the job. It was the first job he'd had in months, and he was happy he'd be able to pay his bills on time. He slept a dreamless sleep.

Carolus woke at 0700 hours. Drove to the spot. He felt lucky that the man liked to swim in a secluded hot spring near his home.

He entered the spring a hundred meters away from a lone figure with his shirt off. Carolus did not undress; the water seeped into his trousers, all the way up toward his crotch and plain T-shirt. Steam rose off the water and filled the sky with small clouds, each one providing cover in the distance so that the only colors were Aster blue and serrated white.

This was not meant to look like an accident, as many clients required. The most popular elimination request was a heart attack. Carolus usually achieved this by dripping his homemade pharmaceutical cocktail onto the mark's tongue during REM sleep. Once he considered trademarking the cocktail and selling it to other contractors, but he quickly thought better of it. Drowning and suicide were a distant second and third. This job, however, was a message. A show of dominance. Carolus enjoyed the theatrics of his work.

From a short distance, he took out his binoculars and made out his mark. Three moles on the back. Bald. He removed his Ruger from his jacket and, with a thump, shot the man twice in the forehead and once in the neck. The mark did not flounder. His body spasmed as each shot thunked his flesh. He splashed into the steaming pool. Carolus commended himself for not making the man suffer. It was always best when they did not have to face their own mortality. Better for him, better for them. Most people couldn't handle knowing they have to die.

You'd think they'd know it from the moment they're born. We spend our whole lives trying to convince ourselves we're immortal, Carolus thought. Who was he to tell this swimming disc jockey he wasn't?

Carolus removed his jacket, tossing it onto the shore, and swam up to the mark to check his pulse. The water boiled on his body and he released, pissing into the warmth of the spring. Carolus worried the act was disrespectful, but he couldn't help it. He'd been holding it for hours. He pressed his index and middle finger against the man's neck. He looked at his eyes: still open as if anticipating something. Carolus felt an uncontrollable urge to speak to him. The mark was not very bloody; he almost looked like he could be listening.

"I've been thinking a lot about this," Carolus whispered, "where I'd want to be buried and how I'd want to be displayed. Shrouded with something pedestrian, like lamb's wool. And the cloth shouldn't be the colors of my flag because I'm really not much of a patriot. I'm constantly touring a place I know nothing about. Finding these women—"

The mark had a pretty little wife who wouldn't find him for at least another few hours. He wished, for her sake, that she stayed at work a little later that night, maybe enjoyed happy hour, anything to delay discovering the horror he'd caused. Carolus sometimes thought about what it would be like to fuck one of the widows he'd created. He could never bring himself to do it—it brought him too close.

The mark's mouth had moved when Carolus shot him in the neck. Carolus wondered why last words meant more than the rest. Probably some words in the middle had been more poignant, more representative of his disc jockey life: *This is mark number thirty-two with a little "Jingle*

All The Way," getting you and yours into that Christmas spirit. Remember: if you're dying in a warm spring somewhere, you're not alone! Wanna give a shout out to all my fellow marks out there. Better luck next time, amigos.

Carolus found his work fulfilling, such as it was. He enjoyed the surgical nature of his own movements, but it burdened him with loneliness. The dull, cragged rock jutted out of the murky burbling water, and the steam blended with the snow so that the forest seemed endless, sterile, and suffocating. Carolus remembered walking through the Reykjavik fish cemetery when he was a boy, their dried and scaly heads dangling above him by the thousands; the place stunk of the sea, death, and his grandmother's stockings after she'd gardened. That same feeling of desolation crept through his body now.

Though the mark's company was little comfort, Carolus floated closer to him. He didn't often linger near the body. He felt almost a perverse enjoyment. Killing had become too ordinary these last few years. This was something new. Careless.

It was against the rules.

In the distance, obscured by the steam, a figure appeared. They held still as if watching him, then disappeared into the trees. If anyone had seen Carolus, life as he knew it was over. There wouldn't be much evidence more damning than a picture of him posing with the man he'd just killed. He dug his nails into his palms.

Panicked, Carolus slashed through the spring out into the freezing air. His hair stood frozen straight, and he raced to where the figure stood, toes squishing inside his boots. The air bit at him, tightened his throat. He found nothing, not even footprints in the snow. He lingered there, searching furiously for a trail. It felt like his sister, Cass, had caught him masturbating in the woodshed all over again—a painful, choking regret and denial. He wondered if he should cry or pray or run, but he just stood there thinking until his crotch grew icy and his pants tightened around him.

It was time to head back, he thought. No sense lingering.

* * *

Carolus had never gotten used to the scent of rotten eggs as he showered. His mother had said it was from the sulfur and that they were lucky to have the hot springs as a free water source. Carolus wished he could buy water that didn't remind him of the living room chair after his Uncle Isturus sat there.

He left the hotel at 0600 hours. At intervals of 200 meters, he tossed each part of his pistol, the silencer, his old shoes, and his blond wig from the car window. He tried to put the figure in the shadows out of his mind. Even if someone was looking, they had been too far to make him out, especially with all the vapor in the air. He repeated it like a dandelion wish. Once for each bleached seed.

He made his way to Wildwood Diner, which was halfway between where he was going and where he'd been. The place was lit up in neon green and pink. Fifties, American-style, glowing yellow from the inside. A metallic boomerang wrapped around an empty parking lot. The customers had all been drinking too much coffee and eating too much pie. It showed in their round, Germanic faces.

There weren't very many workers, so Carolus sat himself at a leather booth to the right of the counter. He wore clean tennis shoes. His palms stuck to the countertop. He removed his jacket and signaled to the pudgy short-order cook whose skin was orange like a tangerine. Maybe he'd been tanning, Carolus thought, since the sun hardly came up at all now. Three hours of sunlight brought a grim state to Reykjavik in the winter. Cubicle workers didn't see the sun for months aside from holy days. They were the first to sustain the pallid melancholia tempered only by the fluorescence of the moon, Roman candles, and seaside bonfires that meant Christmas loomed.

It began to snow.

CHAPTER 2

December 11, Evening

Cass washed dishes the old-fashioned way: her hands snug under blue latex gloves. The kitchen smelled of cloves and lemon. Carolus didn't hear her husband, Bjorn. Maybe he was out, he thought. Bjorn took long walks sometimes after dinner with the Australian cattle dog. He was very fond of the creature. Carolus had often debated the merits of owning a cattle dog in a region with no cattle.

"I met a girl the other day," he said, walking up behind Cass and handing her his empty wine glass.

Cass rolled her eyes. She knew her brother better than anyone. "How can you tell one from the other, Carolus? Was she Polish?"

Cass had grown straight white hair since she was sixteen. Their mother said this was because she didn't eat enough cabbage.

She was only two years older than Carolus, but often cooked for him in the unflinching, copious way their mother would have. Bjorn never liked their close relationship. He worked at a soap shop called Skin in Reykjavik. Carolus sometimes thought of poisoning his soup. He ate large amounts of split pea, which made his bowels an easy target.

"Where's Bjorn?" Carolus asked.

"He went to get the paper," she said, shutting off the faucet.

"It's eight at night."

"He doesn't like to be surprised."

Carolus playfully unzipped the back of her sundress with one swift motion of his hand—like he used to when he was six, and she was eight.

"Zip it back!" she ordered.

"I don't want to!" He often reverted to a childlike state around Cass.

"You know what Mama used to do when you did that."

Their mother had beaten him with a wooden spoon for actions like this, which didn't hurt much, but left small crescents on his arms and neck.

Cass reached her wet, gloved hands around her back and zipped herself up. Her knuckles left thin waterlines on the back of her dress.

"Your husband oughtta buy you some new dresses. You always wear this one." It was a thin, soft blue garment. He liked it.

"Why don't you buy me a dress? Business has been good, you said," she posited, hands buried in suds.

"I don't know your size," he lied, walking into the living room. The area, unchanged since his childhood, glowed burnt orange with a tall oak banister facing the kitchen and an oval table to the right. In the small wall space over the couch and under the banister, fourteen pictures hung. Of them. Of Bjorn by himself, smoking. Of their old dog. Of the cattle dog. Of a child Carolus didn't recognize. Of two figures dancing, barely indistinguishable from one another. Carolus had always suspected the figures were their parents, but had never asked. Now it was too late.

Cass finished the dishes, and Carolus sat on the velveteen love seat.

"You ever hear of a dead pool?" she asked, squeezing next to him. "Bjorn's whole office went in on one."

Carolus yawned. "The whole soap store? They're just so edgy over there, aren't they?" The concept made him think back to an Olympic curler he'd suffocated in his sleep. A dignified surrender, he remembered—something Carolus knew he'd never achieve. There was something very calming about curling. During the Olympics, Carolus would stay up all night watching them sweep the ice. He liked the little jackets they wore.

"They sell potpourri, too. It's a betting pool to see who you think is going to die next!" Cass exclaimed too excitedly. "You never heard of that? That seems like something you'd be into."

"Why's that?" Sometimes Carolus feared death was what defined him, and that Cass, the person he loved most, could never see him as clearly as his marks in that singular moment when their souls left their bodies. He belonged with them, he thought sometimes.

"It's usually with celebrities," Cass said. "Like Helen Mirren. She looks very healthy, but I'll bet you she's about to pop any minute."

"You mean like spontaneous combustion? I'm no good at these things."

Carolus imagined Helen Mirren's body lifting off the ground and bursting like a dropped vase.

Then Bjorn walked in.

He was blond, of course, as all of Cass's other men had been. His nose was far too straight for his asymmetrical face. He wore a baby pouch on his chest for when the cattle dog grew fatigued. This was the clearest sign he did not deserve Cass, Carolus thought. A man should never carry a dog. He should teach the dog to carry him. Carolus was almost sure that came from the Bible.

"There's pickled shark in the kitchen. And soup. I didn't want to make Carolus wait," Cass said.

Bjorn was tall with the body of a swimmer. "It would be tragic," Bjorn said. He removed the cattle dog from his chest and placed it on the floor. It stared at Carolus. They were not fond of each other.

"You should find someone to cook for you," Bjorn remarked.

Carolus looked at Cass. "I think I've got that covered, brother."

"Yes, well, in any case, you might want to start looking outside the family."

Cass got up and kissed Bjorn on the shoulder. "If you two could at least be civil around me, it would be much appreciated."

Carolus checked his watch. It had no numbers. Just a blank face staring back at him in silver. "I have somewhere to be."

"New client?" Cass questioned.

"Yes, how is the importing/exporting business?" Bjorn cross-examined.

Carolus made his way to the door. "You should come watch me work sometime, brother. If dealing in feminine products ever gets you down."

"I'll pass," Bjorn replied, inspecting his cuticles. "You see the wonderful thing about soap is that everyone will always need it. People needed soap before it was invented. You can never have enough soap because it so quickly goes away. Most people don't even know what goes into the making of soap—cold process soap, hot process soap, liquid soap, glycerin soap. It's a beautiful science. Each process changes the consistency, the lather—"

Bjorn snapped up his head, about to continue, but Carolus was already slipping out the front door. He scoffed, shaking his head. "Your brother is an asshole."

"But he's our asshole," Cass called out, her dress still slightly unzipped.

CHAPTER 3

December 12
Stekkjastaur: Sheep Worrier

Carolus recalled the first time his father told him of the Yule Lads. He must have been very little because, in his memory, his father was massive, though Carolus always remembered him as being very large and smelling of leather. His father had been filling up the gas tank of his auburn Renault as Carolus watched from inside, the window slightly cracked.

From the corner of his eye, Carolus saw a small, human-like figure emerge from underneath a rock and scurry across the highway into the deep forest. He quickly rolled down the foggy window to get a better view. The cold stung his eyes. Behind the forest was a jagged, snowy mountain hump, which had turned the color of the sky: Prussian blue.

"What was that?" Carolus inquired.

His father was smoking, and the poorly-shaven man inside the gas mart peered at him. "What was what?" He kept his eyes on the Kroner meter.

"That little man who came out from that rock."

Carolus's father took a long drag and flicked his cigarette toward the building. Straight in the direction of the attendant. "It's probably an elf switching homes."

"What's wrong with his home? Also, what's an elf?"

Carolus's father peered into the car at his son's tiny, expectant face. "Your mother never taught you about the Lads and elves? It's our history."

"She said the Lads are a corporate fabrication made to sell fireworks and twine."

His father smelled like gasoline. His gray chest hair needled out of his white T-shirt. He always dressed like that, even on the coldest days.

Carolus was convinced he was invincible. The boy saw his father as a mountain of a man, someone who could tame a bear, win a medal, drag a semi through the snow. Carolus imagined being like him one day, unafraid of cracks in the ice and the sounds of the radiator.

"Yeah, well your mother doesn't know diddly shit. Don't repeat that," he quickly added. "The Yule Lads are little, you know—Santas. You know what Santa looks like right?"

"Droopy hat?"

"Yeah, basically, except they're . . . specialized." He rubbed his greasy forehead and wiped his hand on his black trousers. "Like they have nasal fetishes. Enjoy milk a lot. Like that. And there's one of them for each of the days of Christmas."

Carolus considered that description. "What's a fetish?"

His father placed the gas nozzle back on the machine and screwed the cap on the tank. He crammed his large body into the car and started the engine. "Kiddo, if you're anything like me you'll figure that one out soon enough."

* * *

Outside, it was sleeting, and the streets were glazed black with ice. The green skies had blown in from the north and settled squarely over Reykjavik. The stars and clouds dripped with a color that would have smudged if it ever crept beneath the horizon. It was impossible to use bridges in times like these because they became brittle and slippery. Once, when Carolus was very young, he witnessed the neighbors' boy slide over one bridge straight into the next town.

As Carolus walked against the molasses winds, ice built in his ears, and the world went strangely silent. At his feet, grungy, lupine mutts tracked his deep boot prints, but they soon became distracted and chased a black rabbit unaware of its bloody fate in the white distance.

Carolus walked by placing one foot in front of the other like he did as a boy. He kept his movements precise because he refused to wear anything but black loafers—the same Hugo Boss pair his father had worn but resoled—when navigating the icy Reykjavik roadside. He was supposed to meet a potential client at Dillon, a rock bar. Carolus liked to meet clients there because it was loud and no one of consequence ever entered the joint. He excluded himself from the assessment. Inside stood three men: hooded, lipsticked in black, their shiny onyx hair and silver chain belts hanging over a brunette in a red dress who seemed to know them.

Carolus set himself at an oak table next to the short bar. The moment between arriving and spotting the client was always tense. Though he had done his due diligence, each meeting contained inherent dangers. This was a local businessman, clean record.

He spotted a man sitting in the booth they'd previously agreed upon. He wore a straw hat. This oddity made Carolus uncomfortable. Nothing should stand out. Carolus survived on attention to detail. But this was business. Business was good. When business wasn't good, Carolus checked the obituaries or the classifieds for anyone who might be seeking some kind of flesh compensation. In some circles injury can only be repaid in blood. Those were Carolus's circles. Those were his best clients.

The bass ached in his chest. He approached the booth, sliding in across from the stranger.

"There's a man in Istanbul—" the client yelled over the music.

Carolus stopped him there. "I'm a local merchant. Do you have any closer vendettas? Maybe Denmark? And take that fucking hat off."

The client reached up and begrudgingly placed his head covering on the table. He didn't seem like a man who was used to taking demands. "I've only got one, and he's a real sonofabitch—somebody you'd really want to see dead." The client looked over Carolus's shoulder for a waitress. Dillon didn't have any, which Carolus liked; there was no one to overhear.

"You ever consider handling it yourself?"

"It hadn't crossed my mind." He licked his teeth. His hair was matted down and wet. He was in his mid-forties, with large eyes like a puma.

"Have you ever watched someone die?" Carolus thought of his mother, alone in her bed, her tiny knit cap sagging down over her eyes. He didn't normally allow his mind to wander when he was with clients.

"Is that the sort of question you ask all your potential customers?"

"You're not buying a car. You're not a customer. You're an accomplice. That means I have to trust you, and you have to answer my questions."

"My wife."

"How did your wife die?"

He shifted in his chair, glancing away. "Cancer."

"Sorry to hear. So, can you imagine this person—this son of a bitch—can you imagine him like that? Knowing you pulled the trigger?"

"I will not pull any triggers."

"I'm the trigger," Carolus growled. He never averted his eyes. His mother had always said his stare frightened people, starting with the other children at school.

"Well, this guy you could imagine," the client said. "I can imagine it." Carolus traced his finger around the cracks in the wood table where his whisky would have been. He didn't drink around clients. It instilled more confidence.

"Look, that would run you, with expenses," Carolus started, converting krona to euro in his head, "Eight hundred thousand euros. It's a long—"

"That's fine. As long as it's done on Christmas."

Carolus was overshooting. He wasn't expecting anything near that. Far more than any other job he'd ever done. He could even think about retiring if he made good investments. A great offer, to be sure. But Istanbul was far. It was so removed from everything—from the waitress with the restaurant on her nose, far from Cass.

The lack of haggling threw him a bit, but he tried not to show it. He tasted the peanut butter he'd eaten earlier. "One hundred thousand on the front end. I'll be in touch with an answer within the week."

"I was told you're a cold-hearted motherfucker. The kind of person who would kill a panda. The kind of person you don't want to run into during tax time. You know what I mean? Am I wrong? Did they have it wrong?"

"They're never wrong," Carolus assured. One of the Goth rockers reached his hand down the girl's red dress. "It's Christmas, you know. Yule Lads and whatnot."

"Yeah, right. Well, I'm not asking you to move—" He put his hat back on.

Carolus thought of Cass and Bjorn—what a smug, gangly man he was. Carolus figured his brother-in-law would always hold it over him if he missed Christmas. Maybe even poison Cass against him. The holiday had carried increased importance since their parents died. "Well, anyway. I like the air here, so I'll let you know," he decided.

"For that you can afford to breathe whatever you like." The client got up and left.

Carolus waited a few minutes. As he got up to leave, he walked past the group of Goths. The girl in red eyed him as if she wanted to be saved from the surrounding men. Everything inside him wanted to take the sheath knife from behind his calf and slit their throats. But Carolus didn't get mixed up in things like that. He also never took jobs killing women. He was a traditionalist. Maybe "Straw Hat" would come back and help her. He seemed like a real fucking philanthropist.

* * *

Carolus thought of Christmases and the nights when the Yule Lads would visit. He would find a small puffin, break its tiny wing, and eat it with the Brennivin sauce his mother made only around the holidays. His mother said it was acceptable to kill the puffins because they had grown, lived lives full of merriment, and already had pufflings of their own.

On December 12, the first day of the visitations, he'd place his best shoe—a small black boot—on the windowsill and wait to see the Yule Lads. He hoped voraciously for a new PEZ dispenser or a horn, but every year on December 13, he'd wake to find a potato in his boot and the window slightly ajar, the cold air coming in making his fingers too cold to peel it.

Stekkjastaur was his least favorite Yule Lad. Carolus never ate the potato.

CHAPTER 4

December 13
Giljagaur: Gully Hawk

By the seaside, the sun rose and set. Solfar the Sun Voyager stood as a celebration of history. It was a sculpture of a mammoth steel Viking ship. Carolus climbed to the top of the skeletal metal that pointed to Reykjavik harbor—a ribbed series of deft metallic strokes. The water always flowed ice blue. He clung to its stern. Below, Carolus inspected the black roots of the waitress's hair. They'd been seeing each other fairly regularly since the night in Grindavik. She traced the path of a ship along the water with her finger.

"You ever hear of a dead pool, Peach Pie?" he asked.

"Sounds like something I should avoid."

A gull landed on a nearby rock and observed the couple. The waitress hoisted herself up on one of the ship's lower rungs.

"It's something that interests me," Carolus revealed.

"Are you often attracted to the morose?" She attempted to get closer to Carolus but stopped short.

Maybe she couldn't climb, he thought. There was something blameless about her face—the way her hair framed it into a circle, the way she brushed it back. Since he was a boy he'd dreamt of dying with a woman, sharing death like orgasms—something he'd seen in a movie when he was too young to be watching it.

"I think everyone is enamored with impermanence," he said after a long pause.

"I once killed my goldfish. I was sad for three weeks."

He grabbed one of the ship's ribs and dangled down toward her so that they were almost touching noses.

"I'm supposed to kiss you now," she said. And she did.

Carolus figured his sister would have cooked salmon and if he hurried he could have some. He allowed himself to fall a short distance to the ground. The waitress immediately straddled him.

"How quickly will you replace me?" she asked.

"How long before you bought another fish?"

"Two weeks," she said. "But it wasn't my idea."

In that moment, Carolus resolved that he wouldn't go to Istanbul. He could make up the money in other ways. It was Christmas, and he only had one piece of family left. He could breathe anywhere, but he'd rather breathe in Reykjavik.

* * *

Carolus thought back to advent midnights when it was hard to sleep because the ice clattered on the windows like silver teeth. His mother would be up too, somehow aware of how important those winters were, of how few there would be to come. She'd boil milk and pour the steaming liquid into a tall glass, then drift off in the living room to the flickering neon tree.

Carolus sat alone in the kitchen, his feet cold but raised up off the ground. His small fingers hovered around the warm glass of milk as if it were fire. He sat on his favorite metal stool. There were three others just like it, but that one was his favorite. Sometimes, he'd have to fight Cass over it because she knew it bothered him.

The kitchen was the color of butter. Faded manila countertops, stove, and dishwasher, urine-colored walls. Moonlight poked through the white curtained window, creating a bright splotch on the flower-patterned linoleum floor. The hollow sound of infomercials emanated from the living room. Something about yogurt spoons.

Carolus remained at the kitchen table, but before he could drink his treat, Giljagaur, the Gully Hawk, appeared and sucked the froth right off the top with his green, silken lips. He wore a bear fur vest and his beard, though mostly deep black, settled gray at his chin. He stood only about one or so meters tall. The haggard, gluttonous look in his eyes said he wanted more.

"That was my froth," young Carolus said.

"Froth is my life," Giljagaur said, licking his pointed front teeth. He searched his tiny corduroy pockets, pulled out some lint and placed it in Carolus's hand. "There."

Carolus recognized him immediately. He had studied the Yule Lads voraciously after learning of them from his father. "Why do they call you the Gully Hawk?" Carolus asked. He searched anxiously for his mother's silhouette.

"Why did you kill that rabbit?"

Days before, Carolus had stalked a small white rabbit through the woods and killed it with a stick and his hands. He had buried it under the snow, but days later, found that ravens had unearthed it and ripped apart its remains. He'd been sure no one was watching, and he felt shame for its discovery. "I'm a hunter, I think."

"Have you ever thought about hunting things other than rabbits?"

"Like foxes? I've thought about foxes."

The Gully Hawk circled behind Carolus, stretching on his long tiptoes so that his thorny beard brilloed against Carolus's cheek. "Do you know how I got in here? Do you know that I watched your mother?"

Carolus's arm hair stood up again, and he felt helpless. The feeling swirled, tightening in his belly. Helplessness often felt like unintended arousal. He drank some of the warm milk.

"Look, boy—I can teach you. I can make you strong." His wrists were the color of wax paper.

"Why?" Carolus wished his feet were touching the ground so he could run. His socks felt suddenly itchy.

The Gully Hawk grabbed Carolus's chin and rubbed his thin fingers over his lips. "Because you'll crave more than rabbits soon enough."

CHAPTER 5

December 14

After eating his typical Sunday breakfast of herring and onions, Carolus decided to go to church. He knelt inside Hallgrim Cathedral. It was radical in its time, with a long beige steeple, tiered by buttresses like organ pipes, looking straight down on Reykjavik. Carolus liked to plant himself at a pew near the confessional and plot out his days. His face still hurt from the cold, although it was one of those nights where the winter felt warm because it had already bitten through.

Mostly, when he knelt in the cathedral, he thought of the rules the Yule Lads had laid out all those years ago when he'd begun his training.

Each of the Yule Lads had a rule, so there were quite a lot of them, some of which seemed overly specific. Nevertheless, Carolus always abided by them because they'd never led him astray.

The Rules:

1. Never steal from a man with a sheep painted on his door, for he is wiser than you.

2. Do not hide in a place where the odor will later reveal your timeline.

3. Never underestimate the unusually small, and do not give any extra credence to the tallest of men.

4. Never kill a woman.

5. Never forget the details. So much that is delicious is often left behind.

6. Always check under the bed.

7. The first thing they will ask is what they heard. You cannot be seen, but also do not be heard.

8. Do not drink on the job. Eat yogurt.

9. Stay calm up until the point of the kill. Never lose your temper before you are prepared to strike.

10. Those closest to you can often become liabilities.

11. Stealing a wife is like stealing someone's pork loin. It is frowned upon.

12. Beware of the man who favors the furry over the skinned.

People probably figured he was praying when he sat there. It helped to know some of the fanatics—the widows who, out of guilt or mourning, forced their tiny withering bodies onto the dark oak of Hallgrim. They'd defend him if anyone ever questioned his moral standing. They were more loyal than God. It wasn't that he didn't believe in religion, necessarily. He believed in sanctity: adhering to ritual, enduring sacrifice, and calling on God to punish. The Lads believed in the sanctity of desire.

He removed his leather gloves and rubbed his reddened ears. An old woman walked by. He had a knack for faces. "Morning Mrs. Kjelld," he whispered. She smiled as if acknowledging their parity in the eyes of the Lord.

Carolus watched his oniony breath rise from his lips and be absorbed into the bulky church rafters.

* * *

He recalled making love to a snow angel on the top of a hill by his house when he was ten. The local children had built enormous castles after the first frost and, hardened by rain, the frozen structure gleamed from a distance. Carolus remembered sneaking out of his backyard, where his mother endlessly shoveled snow from one side to the other. He fornicated with the blustery winter goddesses hidden in the deep folds of the drift.

The thirteenth of December was Giljagaur's day. Carolus hid in wait of the Yule Lad who'd been skulking in the snow gullies, hoping to sneak into the nearby cowshed to steal milk. He looked the same: toucan-nosed and red-hatted, eyes darting like some coked up lizard—this time carrying wooden buckets for his plunder. He wore a belt of frayed rope around his pudgy belly. It reeked of mildew. His fur vest was matted with liquid, heavy and sopping.

Carolus had been waiting for him all year. He'd considered Giljagaur's offer to teach him to hunt. The Lad stopped and acknowledged the young boy. They were both hidden away, a couple of Christmas vandals. That night, they came to an understanding.

"I know what you are," Giljagaur said. "We're the same, but I desire something far less frowned upon."

Carolus rested his cheek on the snow, hidden from his mother who lazily searched for him as dusk approached. He felt the cold straight through to his teeth. "Don't people see you differently? Don't they know about you?"

"I don't hide. I'm proud of my work. It's goddamn tradition. I'm gonna teach you different."

"But I only see you once a year."

"We're all going to help you." Giljagaur unlatched the door to the shed and crept into the darkness.

Carolus remained outside. "The other Yule Lads?" The ice seeped through his sweatpants.

"All I do is swindle," Giljagaur called from inside the shed. "Some of the others—the real sons-a-bitches—they'll teach you how to prey. God, haven't you ever wanted to just thieve a bunch of milk and cover yourself in it like a fucking milk vest?"

"Milk vest?"

"God, there's a fuckshot you don't know yet," Giljagaur said. He emerged from the shed with two sloshing drums of milk, placed them in the snow, and dragged Carolus away by his nostrils for his first lesson.

* * *

Carolus felt he hadn't changed all that much since then. There was only one reason he visited church, and it had nothing to do with repentance. He kept his eyes locked on the confessional. The priest was seventy-six with enlarged balls. When he finally left to piss, Carolus slipped inside the curtain. He lifted up a lead slab on the floor and climbed down a creaky wooden ladder to a long-forgotten fallout shelter beneath the building. It was ironic that so many confessions had been heard above the storage of such menace.

The only reason Carolus even knew about the room was that his middle-school girlfriend's great grandfather built Hallgrim. Her grandfather told her about it four days before he died, terrified that no one would ever find his priceless stamp collection. Once, Carolus touched Sally's stockinged leg in that room, but he was too afraid to kiss her.

The rectangular space was compact and simple. A few crates of canned water, Campbell's soup from the sixties, a bunk bed, a foldout table with a red checkered tablecloth, and a small safe filled the room. His mesh-metal locker contained gun parts, ammo, extra gloves, shoes, coats. It also housed other odds and ends that he'd found useful over the years: cake knives, moonshine, Brillo pads.

It was usually a very safe place. Somewhere he could reflect. But Carolus suddenly felt queasy. The Master Lock to the locker lay severed on the floor. As he swung open the door, his mouth dried up. A note read:

Good seeing you again. I got some lovely pictures of us by the hot spring. Catch you soon, brother.

* * *

Carolus's mind raced. He considered the ways this man could kill him: hanging from a modern art museum flag post or castrated in a fish processing plant. He was worried but excited. Now he had a nemesis. Someone worthy of slaughtering. "Brother." Maybe another contractor, he thought.

Carolus realized his safest spot on earth was no longer secure. He'd have to get out. Leave the country. Leave Cass. The Lads would have agreed.

He snatched his 9mm and dusted the space with a rag, erasing his fingerprints. Foolhardy, maybe. How many times had he been down in that space alone? How many fingerprints had he left in the strangest places? He clicked the combination on the safe to extract his records and heard a hiss. Next to the moonshine, a small fuse lit and, with a tiny spark, the bottle shattered, spewing glass and flames. The flaming liquid washed outward and caught onto the ladder. He swiped the flames off his slacks.

Carolus shoved the pistol under his waistband and scurried up the ladder, the fire burning his toes. He pushed his way up, but the slab wouldn't give. As he climbed the rungs, he smelled burnt leather. He gave a violent heave, knocking over Mrs. Kjelld, who was reciting the Act of Contrition. As he pulled himself up into the confessional, he sealed the lead slab and raked his arm across his forehead, his hair soaked with sweat.

"Everything all right there?" the priest asked through the mesh.

Carolus exhaled. "Forgive me," he panted, carrying limp Mrs. Kjelld over his shoulder through the billowing smoke as he escaped.

CHAPTER 6

Carolus knew that he'd have to stay away for a while, for his sake and his sister's. The job in Istanbul presented a perfect opportunity. The hard part would be telling Cass.

She was sitting by their old sandbox in the backyard when he arrived. Carolus pulled into the driveway and saw her in her little red coat through the metal fence that looked into the back alley. Her figure was bright and clean against the jagged lines of the ice. As Carolus walked toward her, he ran his fingers over the blue wooden front porch. It always seemed as if it could tumble at any moment from the weight of the logs that she'd piled in its corners, the white Christmas lights, and the snow piles she hadn't cleared.

Mother's old metal stool barely peeked over the railing. She'd always said it was good for posture. Her perfume smelled like the sunset.

Small black weeds stuck up through the drift and dotted the snow. Cass teetered on the edge of the frozen sandbox, not knowing she was being watched. She hadn't put on lipstick or combed her long platinum hair. Patches of thin brittle tree trunks, gaunt as shadows, surrounded the yard. Through them, Carolus could see the denim moon although it was only 15:15. It was in the days when the sun never appeared at all that Carolus felt most at ease.

He approached her, looking out onto the tire-rutted roads, exhaust-blackened, yellowed by strays and small directionless wolves.

"You reek," Cass said, leaning back on the ice. "Have you been smoking again?"

He sat down across from her on the sandbox. He hadn't even realized that he must smell of incense, organ musk, and Mrs. Kjelld's burnt gray hairs. Poor woman. He hoped she was all right. He'd just left her on a nearby bench as flames burst the windows and licked the building like bobcat tongues.

"Did you hear about the fire at Hallgrim?" she continued. "It was all over the news."

He looked down into the frozen sand; he saw a squirrel that must have been trapped there all winter, an ashtray filled with Lucky Strikes, olive pits, and gum. "Anybody die?"

"A few old women. Smoke inhalation. It's very sad. What do you care though?"

"What's that supposed to mean?"

Cass chipped some of the paint off her fingernails. "I dunno. Usually, you yell at me for telling you about the news. You say it's a contest to see who can film the most blood."

The cattle dog trotted over from his water dish on the porch and rested his head on Carolus's lap. "Your dog's getting fat," he said.

"Bjorn keeps feeding him ham. He's got very high cholesterol."

"How are things with Old Spice?"

"You're such a little boy sometimes." She paused and thought about it. Her silken white hair stuck to her cold red cheeks. "He takes me roller-skating when I like."

"And in bed?" Carolus asked.

Cass drifted back across the sandbox. "What kind of question is that for your sister?" She shoved his leg playfully.

He enjoyed moments with her when he could be almost completely himself. For him, her love was reassurance that he wasn't beyond repair—not that he wanted to change. Carolus liked the way he worked. His secrets felt like warm chocolate on his gums.

"I'm leaving for Istanbul tomorrow, and I don't want you to come with me."

Shock spread across Cass's face, lips shifting into a long frown that forced two deep lines at the top of her brow. The cattle dog became alarmed. It rose from Carolus's knee and unsuccessfully attempted to navigate the ice under its paws.

Cass settled the dog on her lap in one swift motion as if clearing a plate. "Who'll cook for you?" she asked.

"Turks, I guess."

She thought about it. "Are you leaving because of me?"

He looked at the dog. He wished he could tell her why he was going. That it was for her protection. That if they found out who he was, they could follow him here. Unless he'd already led them to her. He glanced around.

"Are you going to be back in time for Christmas?" she asked as if she were ten again.

"Don't know if I'll be back in time for anything, Cass."

The heat from her bottom made small incisions in the ice. Sand bubbled up from underneath, turned the surface murky.

"But who will make the apple sauce?" she posed.

Carolus thought of how he always made the apple sauce for all family functions. His uncles used it on their meat, and Cass displayed it like a prize.

"I absolve myself of the apple sauce," Carolus said. He placed his hands down in the snow behind him. The cold shot through his body.

"Well, we'll just have to have Christmas without you," Cass groaned, trying to lift herself off the ice. "But Mom wouldn't have wanted this."

"You're going to guilt trip me now? She's dead. I doubt she wants anything."

"You're coarse sometimes." Cass rose up. "You talk about her like she's not still with us. I feel her all the time."

Carolus remembered going through the alphabet with his mom as she mouthed words. She could still nod then. Sometimes she'd drift off as he went through, and they'd have to restart. Most of the time she just wanted water even though she was already getting liquid from the viscous sack hanging above her like a storm cloud.

"Don't you have anything to say?" Cass demanded, cradling the cattle dog with one hand and clutching the half-open screen door with the other.

Carolus reached into his pocket, extracted a cigarette, and lit it. He shook his head and lowered himself into the sandbox. The screen door clattered shut.

CHAPTER 7

December 14
Stúfur: Itty Bitty

Carolus knew he should say goodbye to the waitress. He stopped by Prikid, and when she saw him by the window, she took a cigarette break. The bartender watched them through the window. She kissed Carolus and clumsily lit a Salem. Her lips quivered around it, and he wished he didn't have to leave. It seemed that every desire took a back seat to his work.

"I'm going away," he started, sparking his cigarette on hers without asking.

"To where?"

"It's better if I don't tell you." Carolus's breath poured out like dragon fire.

"Why should I care?" She crossed her arms over her white blouse, trying not to shiver.

"I don't know. I just think you do. Like I do."

She deliberated for a moment. The frost rushed up her back, and she tensed as if discerning a punch line from a joke told years ago. "So you want to screw before you go?"

"I hadn't thought about that," he said.

"Sure you have."

He liked the way her lipstick printed deep red on the filter. There was something inviting about a woman who smoked so forcefully. He wished he could throw her up against the storefront, lift her skirt, and have his way with her right there in the cold in front of all the diners. He wondered if they'd stay and eat.

"Maybe I have," he said. "But I just thought I should tell you, Peach Pie." He liked that she was well-read, something his mother had wished for him. She knew old Russian and Polish literature best and would quote old Soviet writers like Bulgakov as easily as smoking a cigarette. There was a cat in that novel, too. He'd had his own trouble with cats.

"Well, that's real civil of you. And I don't like when you call me that."

"I didn't know," Carolus said, tossing his smoke against the side of the building. He leaned in to kiss her. She bit down on her cigarette, baring her teeth, and went back inside.

* * *

Carolus lingered in front of Prikid, recalling the Yule Lad Stúfur's gritting teeth wedged between the whites of his beard. The other Lads called him Itty Bitty. He wore brown mittens and spoke with a growl that did not suit his stature. His head barely reached Carolus's waist.

"Gil tells me you're interested in honing your senses. That true?" He stood pantless in Carolus's kitchen with only his mittens and matching fur to hide himself.

"I guess so—if Giljagaur said that. Why are you naked?" young Carolus inquired.

"That's really none of your business," he said, scraping the meaty remains off a frying pan. "I'm going to teach you to use your senses to stalk and evade." He scraped voraciously with his blackened fingernails at the last of the pan scraps.

"Do you want something from the fridge?"

"This is the good stuff. You can learn a lot from what people leave behind."

Now, Carolus made his way to Selfoss on the outskirts to visit Samsa, his arms dealer and advisor. Samsa was the kind of man who always seemed out of breath, even while sitting. He had a large belly that extended beyond his formidable chest and a thick scar over his left cheek from the Rainbow Warrior Tour of the late seventies. This was the three-day campaign against Greenpeace Whale Conservationists, a campaign the Icelandic military eventually lost.

Spoon Licker first introduced Carolus to Samsa, though any time he brought it up Samsa denied it. Besides the Lads, Samsa was the only living person who knew Carolus's vocation. In a way, it was comforting to know he was less alone.

The old veteran lifted himself off his torn leather recliner and greeted Carolus by patting his shoulders from the side, not the top. It was a sign of respect. A sign that they were equals—at least that's how Carolus took it.

Carolus took a long drag of his Lucky Strike. "I just need these items to meet me in Istanbul." He handed Samsa a list on a loose-leaf sheet. The list included a Ruger and silencer, his preferred tools.

"Of course you do. I hear Istanbul is full of meat and hookers this time of year."

"That true?"

Samsa kept a collection of taxidermized heads above his couch. There were Indigenous breeds—a cross fox and a grey seal among them—that he'd gotten for 1,000 krona at a garage sale.

"Drink?"

Carolus held his hand open. Samsa poured a Macallan neat and placed it in his palm. The basement was secluded and dark, with a chain light and boxes labeled "monocles" and "socks," as if he'd just moved in. But they were not monocles and socks. Those were the goods: silencers, bullets, and wigs. He also kept a mini fridge, a kitchen table (though he didn't have a kitchen), a recliner with a hollowed-out arm for cash, and a single firearm. From the recliner, he spent his time watching Bravo on an old black and white Sony he'd wired for cable. He said the colors hurt his eyes.

Samsa was the closest thing Carolus had to a friend. He sat at the table and drank his scotch.

"I remember when you first came in here." Samsa got sentimental with booze in him. "I thought you were a pussy."

"You ever been followed?"

"Why? You get followed here?" Samsa tinkled the ice in his glass anxiously.

"Forget it," Carolus said, thinking back to the first time he'd came.

He'd had the urge to shit as Spoon Licker pushed him to Samsa's back entrance. Spoon Licker liked to wear leather jackets and hang out in all-night laundromats. People seemed to gravitate toward him, but he made Carolus uneasy.

"This is the guy to get you started," Licker drooled out. "He's got everything you need to become a bona fide, grade-A, motherfucking force of nature." That's how Spoonlicker talked. Simple was never better.

"How am I supposed to pay him?"

"Well, you're in lotsa big time luck, Carollissimo. He's got something he needs you to do."

"Nothing sexual, right?" Carolus asked.

Spoon Licker straightened his collar and smoothed out his white goatee. "Just smile for the camera."

Carolus looked up at the security cam mounted above the steel-frame door in the backyard. It seemed so out of place; the camera looked like it was worth more than the house. Samsa's property lay on the border of the National Park. Trees surrounded the land on all sides, save for the tiny slit where the red gravel road poked through. Carolus felt vulnerable. It was the first time he'd left Reykjavik.

Samsa was fitter back then. His face wasn't as blotchy, and he seemed, if not happy, at least content.

"You look like a fucking embryo," he said. Licker had disappeared when the door opened.

"I'm fifteen," Carolus admitted.

"Well, what the fuck do you want?"

"Work. No women." Carolus looked around for Licker. He'd delivered the line just like Licker told him to, but he didn't see the Lad anywhere.

"Fuck are you looking for? I doubt you'd even know a woman if she ran into your dick." He paused for a moment and looked Carolus over. "You the killing type?"

* * *

Carolus finished his whisky and placed the glass beside him on the table. "I might not be back for a while," he said.

"I'll miss you, honey bunny. Heard about the fire."

"Yeah, what'd you hear?"

"I thought no women." Samsa dug his fat fingers into the flaking leather.

"Wasn't me. Anyway, someone's onto me."

"Fuck you doing here then?"

He remembered his mother shushing him like the voice of the snow. "Just saying my goodbyes."

"You're gonna be saying goodbye to me a lot sooner than you'd like if you brought anybody here." Samsa pushed up off his chair and checked the door cam.

"If this guy wanted me dead straight off, he would've taken me out in the church. He's playing. He wants to show me he's better. I know how these sick fucks work."

"Cause you're one?"

"That hurts my feelings." Carolus tinkled the ice in his glass toward Samsa. "So, you think I should go?"

"Istanbul?" Samsa leaned hard against the table below the camera view. He picked up the bottle of Macallan. "If this guy is willing to trail you there, it's a real vendetta. No cute shit. You find out who it is and slit his throat before he decides to stop fucking around."

"You think I should be worried?"

Samsa poured Carolus another two fingers before lumbering back to plop into his chair. He groaned. "You should be goddamn terrified, but knowing your twisted fucking tinker, you're probably excited."

Carolus liked that Samsa knew so much about him. He held up his glass. "I'll only stay for six more."

Samsa smiled. "Don't do me any fucking favors."

CHAPTER 8

December 15
Þvörusleikir: Spoon Licker

When Carolus stepped onto the train in Brussels, he walked the entire length of the passenger vehicle, as he often did to form a mental blueprint. In the back, the Renaissance Sleeper: deluxe and standard rooms for the affluent and moderately rich. Next to it was the Manor car: a room for caged animals, mostly talking birds. Then the Chateau Sleeper where he'd be staying: public shower, bathrooms, bedrooms, and a drawing room for artists and jugglers. And finally, the car in which he'd spend the most time: the corporate-sponsored Nutella Car. It contained the smoking lounge adjoined with the kitchen, which didn't seem altogether sanitary. Attached to the dining room was a small staircase that extended from the smoking area to a scenic dome that bubbled over the roof of the train. It seemed meth addicts had taken to this space. It was best to leave them be.

From the outside, it was a replica train—the kind with buttermilk smoke derived from small round tablets found at hobby shops. He shared a compartment with a small Indian family. He felt cramped.

Though they were seated directly across from him in a row, they each approached him separately and introduced themselves. The youngest was a girl named Narula, whose accent was more British than her parents'. Carolus often found her staring up at him when he lifted his eyes from his paper as they sat in the blue leather seats with fake wood trimming. The mother and father introduced themselves as Mr. and Mrs. Pem. He said his name was Boston.

While the train never actually stopped, it slowed down when it reached Belgian towns to let people carrying lattes and hats hop on.

The Pem's, apparently, did not sleep and liked snacking on unsalted crackers and taffy. The girl was looking at him again. Purple-suited ticket takers passed the glass door. A mystical instrumental that sounded like the ocean at night tinkled from the compartment next to his.

Mrs. Pem drew the landscape as it rolled past. Every once in a while, she would show it to the girl. Because she was too accurate or too slow, every color and tree and blade of grass blended into one another and became a single brown smudge.

"Have you heard the news?" Mr. Pem asked after several hours of silence. It was funny, Carolus thought; he was just about to ask if he could smoke.

"Mind if I smoke?"

"It's not good for the girl," he said, glancing at his daughter.

"That's all right," Carolus said. "What news?"

"I was wondering. I haven't gotten any news. Not since getting into Brussels."

"Well," Carolus was about to say he didn't know either, but he looked down at the paper in his hands, "looks like Bobby Fischer died. Right in Reykjavik. Isn't that something?"

"I heard about that already."

Carolus allowed a moment of silence. "Do you go on a lot of trips together?" Carolus looked at Narula.

"More than we do apart," Mr. Pem said. "She's very attached to us, and we encourage it."

"I can't imagine what it would be like to have a girl," Carolus said. But he did imagine it, having a girl who looked a little like him. He would have to scold her and measure the length of her skirts. Nowadays skirts are too short, he thought, and he imagined her wearing a very short garment and trying to sneak out of the house. He was mad just thinking about it. Plaid.

The Euro rail was something Carolus always said he would explore when time and sex permitted. He now found himself without either, though he had a bit more time than he had originally thought. The client needed the job done by Christmas, so Carolus decided he would finish the kill and spend the holidays overseas. He needed to stay out of Reykjavik for a while.

He imagined all of the things that would have a profound effect on his New Year's, though it was still two weeks away:

The *wallet* that would be stolen by the old Iranian women who slept in the corner of his motel room.

The *room key* that would lead him into a tunnel of unclaimed body parts.

The *Absinthe* that would inspire him to poison the husband of a beautiful barista, only to learn the man was not her husband.

Amy-Lou—the beautiful barista.

The *panda bear* who would teach Carolus the value of family and repentance.

He had never met anyone named Amy-Lou, and it seemed about time.

Carolus excused himself and stepped between cars to smoke. The train headed east. The scenery of small pastry villages turned to ash trees and sandal huts, then ruins and back to trees. Finally, it dissipated into long stretches of unreflective, flat water where a city appeared, its rooftops spun with avocado and lace.

Wood planks painted to resemble iron linked the space between the dining and smoking cars. Carolus smoked without his hands and allowed the wind to catch the ash from his lips.

He looked through the cloudy glass into the café car where two boys drank and stared up a woman's blue dress. She was brunette. Her face was angular and sharp with three moles at the bottom of her cheek. Her arms resembled two uncooked hams.

A man-eating sturgeon noticed Carolus taking long drags, letting smoke out the sides of his mouth.

He entered the café car.

That's when Carolus smelled something distinctly of childhood— coffee with goat's milk. He felt the presence of his father in a way he hadn't in over a decade. His coffee had always been cold because he'd left it sitting in the car. It was always too sugary, even for a child. Small mountain sheep would sometimes come up to the window and sniff it.

The sliding door opened behind him. Carolus swung around as fast as he could. He'd always hoped to be stabbed in the front or not stabbed at all. A blunt, flashing pain from behind struck him, knocking him unconscious.

* * *

When he woke, the world had changed colors. Had Carolus never experienced black coffee and purple-suited ticket takers, he would have thought everything was perfectly fine. The sky was no longer blue, but maybe it never was.

A mustached man hovered over him like a doctor, checking his ears. Carolus sat up.

"We thought we'd lost you," the man said. "You were struck by an object of significant girth."

"How long was I out?" Carolus asked.

"Almost two minutes—maybe three. My watch is broken. Excuse me," he remarked as he got up and headed toward the cigarette car. The teenagers and the woman in blue had left.

Carolus went between the cars to get some air. Outside, the grass glowed tangerine, and the trees and the small horses that punctured the countryside took on a dull brown. The sky leaked black.

He took a breath and walked into the smoking car in search of the doctor. Three to four robust men sat at each of the circular tables on either side of the lime-carpeted aisle. They smoked Davidoff's and long cigarettes, each one holding his tobacco differently as if attempting to distinguish himself in the haze. They dressed far too neatly for the scene, and Carolus found it strange that such men existed—trapped sixty years in the past, congregating like geese. They seemed to feed off the smoke, and it created small crest-like halos around their balding heads. Their attention had turned to the opposite end of the car where one woman lay triumphantly as if she'd just seduced a bishop.

"Did anyone see who did this?" He patted the back of his head for blood, but there wasn't much. No one in the car turned to answer him. The backs of their heads said they didn't care. He took a few steps down the aisle. He could see the woman more clearly now. Blonde and smoking in only a see-through silk blouse, black pencil skirt, and black stockings. She paid careful attention to her thin cigarette, which she only puffed when it was about to extinguish, as if teasing it.

"Excuse me," Carolus said. "Did you see who attacked me?" Standing over her, he realized how graceful her presence was and felt an infantile urge.

She didn't look at him, but pointed her cigarette to the next car. A thin film grew over the world like a dirty camera filter. It felt as if he couldn't really touch anything because it might shatter and leave him in purgatorial blankness. He wondered what Spoon Licker would have done, though there was no way he could lick himself out of this situation. There was something far beyond his expertise at work. Carolus hesitated to leave her side, but he had to find out who'd done this to him.

In the next car, he found a woman holding a football trophy.

The woman was much shorter than Carolus and wore a navy vest over a red shirt. She wore her black hair short like a boy's, and her angular features gave her the look of a former athlete. Blood coated the football trophy's marble base. It read Tomas Grumson, second place. The name sounded familiar, but he couldn't place it.

"Did you hit me with that?"

The woman inspected Carolus as if he were a rare vegetable. She examined his face with such intensity that it seemed she was counting each and every imperfection. "This is very possible," the woman said, breaking from her trance.

Her accent reeked of Eastern Bloc. Carolus was unsure how to respond. Certainly he couldn't get any train crew involved. He'd always been so careful to stay out of bar fights and traffic altercations. He'd have to attempt to diffuse the situation, appeal to this woman's rational side. "Well, you can't just go around hitting people with trophies."

"Should I be hitting them with some other item?" the woman asked.

"No. But really a trophy wouldn't be ideal, anyway." He would have chosen something heavier.

"Well, I apologize. I should have struck you with something more typical."

"Listen—who's that lady in there?"

The woman paused very gravely. She picked a purple speck out of her teeth. "This is my wife. She has never cheated on me if that is what you are pondering," the woman said, rubbing the trophy.

"It wasn't—necessarily." Carolus felt sick at this news. Also, he'd probably sustained a concussion. Hearing that this strange, trophy-wielding person had obtained the beautiful woman in the other car made him curious.

"Anyway, why'd you hit me?" Carolus found himself wedged between the door and the woman.

"I thought you were looking like someone else. Allow me to extend my apologies all over you."

"I'd rather you didn't," Carolus said, searching the woman's black eyes—though judging from the sky before, they were probably blue. Maybe he *was* looking like someone else.

"Astrid," she said, introducing herself. "Where are you sleeping?"

Carolus found himself intrigued by his assailant. Maybe it was the blow to the head, but perhaps he could learn something from this woman. Maybe this accident had happened for a reason. Though fate, he thought, is usually subtler.

"Carolus," he said, forgoing his alias. "I'm with a little Indian family a few cars down."

"Well, you must stay with my wife and me. We are having far too much room for ourselves, and she greatly enjoys company."

Carolus smiled at that thought. A ticket taker opened the door behind him and squeezed by, unsettling the delicate balance between him and Astrid.

"It is fewest I can do," Astrid said, holding up the football trophy.

Carolus realized that a move might look unusual, and he shouldn't draw attention to himself. He was tired of the old ways, the Christmas Lads' ways: always regimented and solitary. Why should he be without company on such a long trip, especially when he had a chance to sit in the same room as that beautiful blonde?

"Sure, I'll join you."

Astrid smiled as if she already knew that would be his answer. She asked her wife to get Carolus's bag.

"That's not necessary," Carolus said.

"She has to do things sometimes to stay out of trouble," Astrid said.

Carolus held up his hand. "I prefer to carry my own things."

"We are two compartments past the dining car on the right." Astrid and her wife slid open the door and disappeared down the long body of the train.

When Carolus entered his quarters, he found only little Narula. He sat down across from her. Her eyes glowed orange and her hair seemed white, like Cass's. He wondered what color Cass's hair would be now.

"Are you leaving?" the girl asked.

Carolus nodded. "You'll have this room all to yourselves," he said.

She was starting to get little brown hairs above her lip which she did not yet know she should trim. "My mother says you are the kind of man to watch out for."

"She's probably right."

"Well, I like men like you." She edged up on the bench as Carolus got up with his bag.

"It's funny how that works." He imagined the feeling of her mustache against his beard.

Carolus took his bag and went back through the dining car's lime-green aisles, glancing at the black sky and orange grass outside the smoking car. Astrid's wife had retreated to their living space. He walked through each car looking for them.

Teenagers ate juniper pies and couples conducted grave conversations in confessional positions. In one compartment, a priest and a pregnant girl dressed in all brown held hands and looked anxiously at Carolus as he walked by. Who was he to judge?

Astrid and her wife did have a fairly large compartment. They'd decorated it with miniature religious figures. When Carolus entered, he realized the figurines were poseable. He picked up Jesus and molded him so that it looked like he was running. Running from what? he wondered.

Before speaking, Carolus looked over the large Joseph and Mary sitting in tiny lawn chairs. Thomas Moore held a honey pot that must have belonged to a little Buddhist Winnie the Pooh somewhere else in the room. He grabbed a bowling Confucius and held it to Astrid.

"You enjoy them?" Astrid asked.

Carolus hadn't even noticed that Astrid's wife was now dressed in a slinky silk gown, reading *The Master and Margarita*. She leaned over onto the small table in the middle of the compartment.

"Why do you have them?" Carolus asked.

"It is my business. I create religious action figures. Very big money."

Carolus sat on what would be his bed and leaned on the pillow. He looked at what seemed to be Noah golfing with a couple of zebras and Buddha in a tennis outfit.

Astrid gestured to her wife. "My best seller. This is Delia. She is not for sale." She laughed at her own joke, but Delia did not.

It was tough not to look at Delia's legs. Not a single bruise. Women bruise easily, Carolus thought.

When the train rumbled, some figurines fell from their perches, popcorning, seesawing on the floor. Astrid nudged her wife, who then lifted her head from the book.

"I'll let you two speak." Delia's voice was smooth and light. It was the kind of voice you want to hear in your sleep. Carolus and Astrid both watched her as she left. Her hips swung like Jessica Rabbit's.

There really was a lot of space in the car. Carolus wondered how they could afford such extravagance with such an odd business, despite Astrid's monetary claims. Delia's scent lingered in the cabin. She smelled of clean sex—the kind they show in fifties' movies when women left one foot on the hotel carpet.

Astrid tossed aside Delia's book. "My mother always said a woman like her is not for the keeping. But how do you discard such an ass, you know?"

Carolus nodded. He wondered why his mother had never imparted such wisdom. Cass was full of it. "I'm probably not the one you want to talk to about women."

"You," Astrid said, holding up a Mahatma Gandhi for inspection, "you are just the man I want to talk to." She swung Gandhi's "action fasting arm," and his foam belly receded.

The door slid open. A tall Arab man in a mauve shirt casually entered the room. He paused in the doorway, looking over Astrid and Carolus. He had a hooked chin and lips like two coffee straws. Carolus wondered if Astrid had invited someone else to stay with them.

After a moment of contemplation, the door clicked behind him. Without warning, he removed a barber's razor from his coat pocket and swiped down at Carolus, narrowly missing his throat and crushing the tray table. Carolus grabbed his arm as the assailant forced the razor close to Carolus's neck. They struggled on the cot. Sweat poured down their red faces. Their veins protruded. All of the Arab's weight pushed down on Carolus, and he felt the man's hip dig into his belly. Carolus wondered what it would taste like to be stabbed—maybe like the snow outside Reykjavik that was crisp and white where no one could touch it.

The Arab slid a razor tucked into his palm up to his fingers. Carolus grabbed his wrist, but the blade was already inches from his face. The razor slowly descended on Carolus. He could smell the cheap metal. It balanced just a sliver above the beads of sweat on his face. His forearms shook from the pressure. His heartrate doubled. He knew he couldn't hold out much longer. He closed his eyes, imagining what it would be like to be blind.

The razor pierced Carolus's flesh, and a line of blood ran down his stubble. He thought of a very quiet time when he and Cass ate popsicles and because it was late and warm and the sun stayed out until nearly twelve. He remembered his mother's veiny hands. Without a sound, Astrid rose from the bed and struck the assailant on the crown of his head. The stranger wavered, rolled off Carolus, and wobbled upright, waving the razor. He seemed confused, staring blankly at Astrid as if he'd forgotten she was in the room.

Astrid pulled a tiny poseable Jesus from her blazer pocket and held it out like a vampire's cross. The Arab smirked and lunged at her. Swiftly, Astrid flipped the head off of the poseable Jesus, revealing a knife. She reared back and jammed the tiny figurine into the man's right eye. His flesh squelched and he gasped. The Arab stumbled back, gurgled, slammed against the sliding doors, and crashed to the ground, convulsing.

Carolus nodded to Astrid. He'd been surprised and hadn't reacted quickly. It was possible that Astrid had saved his life. Carolus reached behind her and grabbed rubber gloves from his bag. He pulled shut the plastic curtains on the sliding door, kneeled down, and pried the razor from the stranger's hands. His pulse wound down to a low thump. The Arab would be dead within minutes. Carolus snapped the poseable Jesus from the man's eye socket, pressed it to his throat, and slit it. He despised unnecessary suffering. Astrid watched him work.

Carolus felt an affinity for fellow contractors and didn't like seeing them die. It reminded him that he was not immortal like the Lads. Before a job, Carolus had a way of convincing himself that his mark deserved execution. He had no idea who this man was, though.

Carolus thought back to the first time he saw Spoon Licker's tongue. It was fibrous and muscular, an impressive organ that resembled a girthy whip more than a licking instrument. He remembered Spoon Licker's penchant for wooden spoons, and Carolus appreciated that the Lads were beings of a different time—those who didn't belong in the modern world. It was very disturbing to watch Licker in his kitchen, feeding off an old yogurt spoon his sister had used the night before. He wondered if Licker could taste Cass.

* * *

Carolus's heart thudded in his chest again. The blood pooled in the Arab's eye. It was strange to him that color was such an important part of identifying objects and concepts. Grass was no longer green and thus ceased, somehow, to be grass. Astrid's eyes glowed black like a bat's.

He remembered when he stole a horse in Reykjavik that belonged to his girlfriend's father and rode it into the mountains. He ate Gorgonzola and drank Fresca for three straight days until his nose bled from the cold and he had to turn back and explain his actions.

His world was red then, too—red Gorgonzola and ice and milk. He'd gotten used to a red world when everyone else saw white.

"You are looking comfortable with a corpse," Astrid said.

Carolus jerked his head around. "You're handy with a knife."

"Daughter of a butcher."

The Arab's throat gurgled.

"So, who the fuck are you?"

"I feel that we are both owing new identities, Mr. Carolus," Astrid said. She got up and peeked outside. "The sun descends."

From the base of the Jesus, Carolus watched liquid pour down the Arab's lips and onto his shirt, tie, and blazer. He died urbanely, Carolus thought.

"I have no knowledge of where to place bodies such as this. But I own a factory in Prague," Astrid said. "Perhaps we can refuge there."

"Most people would want the police," Carolus said.

"I prefer to handle things without men in hats."

"Make a lot of enemies in the religious doll business?"

"Who knows these things? Perhaps I slept with his wife and his daughter. Perhaps I sold his family home in Morocco. These things, they run together. I wish my brother was still living around. He always was the good one."

Carolus grabbed the body under the armpits. Using the legs, he shoved it under his bunk and placed his bag in front. "What happened to your brother?"

"Perhaps this is not the time," Astrid said, handing Carolus a kerchief for his bloody neck. There was a knock at the sliding doors.

"Delia?" Astrid asked.

"Refreshments," a voice answered.

"Not now."

"Refreshments."

Carolus rubbed some of the blood out of his beard and cracked open the door. It was a girl of maybe seventeen with pigtails and a figure-hugging vest. Carolus opened the door a little wider. "What color is that?"

The girl looked down. She inspected her chest and then peered back up at Carolus.

"Purple?"

"It doesn't look purple to me," Carolus said.

She looked over herself again as if she might have been mistaken. "No, it's surely purple. I'd bet my life on it."

"Probably not a good bet to make with me." Carolus looked through her and imagined what she would look like as a pretty little corpse. It upset him to think of women that way, but he couldn't help himself.

She shivered in the doorway, turned half away from him. "Refreshments?"

Carolus grabbed the tea and water and mints. He closed the door. Astrid lay back on her bed, sighing. "I must look in on Delia."

"I'll check," Carolus said. "Stay here."

* * *

Carolus found Delia giving out tarot readings to a couple of Parisian accountants who didn't give two shits about their future. They couldn't take their eyes off her breasts long enough to look at her lips or her eyes as she spoke. Even when she told them they would die of terrible fecal diseases and live out their days in lonely boxes on the Seine, they slipped her euros and told her she was right and that they were ready to die.

Carolus grabbed her arm and excused them from the group.

"Coc bloc," they said in dripping French accents. Carolus rarely tolerated the French, and if he were not already in such a terrible situation, he would have put out his cigarette on their chest hair. Chest hair, Carolus thought, should be reserved only for those who've grown it through lovemaking or bloodshed.

He brought Delia outside. Her eyes glowed copper. Twisted black houses owned by mud-soaked farmers and their mangled livestock sprouted along the countryside, and the wind blew through the train so that Carolus felt it in his waist.

"You're costing me drinking money," Delia said, poking Carolus's chest playfully.

"Astrid needs to see you," he said.

"I think Astrid sees enough of me. What do you think?"

"She's starting to grow on me."

Delia tweezed a cigarette from between her breasts.

"How many do you have in there?"

"I can see your little mind racing." She lit up.

"Someone just tried to kill me," he said.

She hesitated for a moment, taking a long drag. "Well, he seems not to have done his job."

"You don't find it odd that your wife was almost just murdered?"

"You never mentioned anything about Astrid. You seem to be fine, so let's get on with it, no?"

Carolus had always dreamed of a woman who could appreciate his work. He noticed a cross hidden beneath the cigarettes, dangling from a platinum necklace deep within Delia's cleavage. "What religion are you?"

"It is so boring when people say what they are thinking when they are thinking it. I'll check on Astrid. Meet me in the smoking car in fifteen minutes." She walked away.

Carolus was hungry from the stabbing and craved pork. He went toward the dining car. Pork was the best food to have after stabbings, just as chicken was for strangling and lasagna for poisoning.

As he was about to sit, he noticed the refreshments girl bending over in the corner as she attempted to stack sandwiches. Her ass had taken the shape of a delicious pear. He wondered if being on a train all her life made her feel well-traveled or like a missing piece in a Ferris wheel.

She made her way over, a notepad in her hand. "What will you have?"

"I'd like you to sit."

She lifted her little brown cap that, until this moment, he hadn't noticed she was wearing. "Sir, I'm not allowed to sit with the customers."

"I'm not a customer," he said, rubbing his neck and wondering if the bleeding had stopped. He could always say it was from shaving. A few droplets came off on his fingers.

"What are you?"

"I own this goddamn train. Now take a seat," he barked.

She sat, convinced by his tone.

"Do you know anything about the women in compartment thirty-seven?" Carolus inquired.

She thought about it for a moment. "They've got a lotta weird dolls and stuff. Is that what you mean?"

Carolus looked down at his blank watch. "I have to go. At the next stop, I want you to stop by that compartment and tell the small short-haired woman, 'Carolus has left.'"

"That's it?" she asked.

"That's it. And just come to the smoking car and tell me what she says." He slipped her twenty euros and ordered the pork. "Oh, and I'll take the biggest knife you have. Train pork is always a bit tough."

In half an hour, Carolus found Delia in the smoking car.

"You're late," she said.

"You didn't seem like a woman who'd be on time," Carolus said, fingering the steak knife in his pocket that he'd swiped from lunch. The car filled with scents of caramelized onions and bean soup from the kitchen next door.

"Why did you accept the offer to stay in our room after the incident?"

"You, mostly," he said.

"But I don't know you."

"That's when women find me most desirable."

She smiled and looked out the window. They approached a tunnel. "Had you ever killed someone before this?"

"Yes, but I can't take all the credit." He hated himself for his candor. He couldn't help it; he wanted to reveal secrets to her.

"And did it feel different this time?"

"It feels different now." Around him, colors began to fade. His sight deteriorated.

"It's silly to think we can be anything but what we already are." Her face lit up and then suddenly went into shadow as they passed through the tunnel. It wasn't like in old movies where everything got dark. Even in black and white, her eyes were mint and hazel and tequila blue. The cabin lights were still on, but Delia now rested her head on his shoulder. It was as if they'd come to the end of a long journey. Her hair smelled of black currant.

"Do you think it is possible, if the situation were to be different, that we could be friends?"

"From the moment I saw you I decided we couldn't," Carolus said.

She kissed him on the cheek. He savored her wet red lipstick.

"I suppose we are either destined to be lovers or star-crossed enemies," she said flatly.

"I'm fine with both."

"I cannot live in these gray areas."

A moment passed between them, and Carolus desperately wanted to touch her hair, but he remained still. They passed a ginger sky where a windmill sliced the clouds into smoke. A small village overrun by mustangs hid under the cover of mountains.

She lifted her head from his shoulder. "I suppose we are enemies then." She smiled the smile Carolus had only seen during Sunday mass. A look of disobedience flashed across her face.

"Astrid is a decent woman," he said.

"So you are not going to try and kiss me?"

At that moment, the refreshments girl walked over. She consulted a notepad. "I've got it. Astrid says, 'I doubt this. Now why don't you . . .'" she hesitated, "'show me those tits'?" she whispered. She looked at Delia, perhaps knowing that she was Astrid's wife and that she might have been more sensitive.

"That's helpful. Thank you," Carolus said, slipping her another twenty euro.

"I'll be around here if you want me," the girl said and walked away.

"She likes you," Delia said. "Why spy on my wife when you can spy on me?"

Carolus shifted in his seat hungrily. "We need to take care of our business at the next stop."

"In Prague," she said. "Astrid's factory is in Prague."

CHAPTER 9

December 16
Pottasleikir: Pot Licker

Disposing of bodies always reminded Carolus of burying cats. He'd never owned one because his mother said they were antisocial and would teach him bad habits. He'd never learned one bad thing from a cat, he thought.

Sometimes he fed strays that would otherwise starve in the winter. Often, they died anyway from loneliness or wolf bites. Carolus remembered their tiny feet and how small they seemed against the vast fields of snow. Sometimes he'd find them still breathing. He would dig shoebox graves while they were just barely alive, praying over their small, soft bodies as they passed in the cold.

He thought about Cass and how Christmas was approaching. He wondered if she was still mad. He should call, but realized he'd already been uncharacteristically reckless on this trip. He'd abided by the Lads' rules all these years; it was time to make some of his own.

Carolus was glad that he didn't have to wash the dishes twice anymore like when he was seven. The thought of Pot Licker's tiny reptilian tongue on his plate was horrible.

He'd emptied out Astrid and Delia's suitcases and placed parts of the Arab in each of them, lining them with latex he'd packed. "It always pays to carry latex and a spoon," Pot Licker lectured. He had long brown hair like a horse's mane and wore gray socks up to his knees. They smelled of fungus and soup.

"And what are *you* carrying?" Delia asked.

"I got us a knife, chopped up this Arab, and eliminated the evidence so your wife isn't wanted for murder. I'm carrying my clothes," Carolus replied. Of course, there were useful tools other than clothes in his bag, but she didn't need to know that. Not yet, anyway.

Delia handed him her toothbrush and a pair of silvery lace panties. Or anyway, with Carolus's strange vision, they looked silverish. "For tonight," she explained.

Astrid's eyebrows furrowed and she leaned over as he stuffed Delia's panties in his bag. "Take these, too," Astrid said, handing Carolus a large pair of discolored cotton underwear.

He quickly shoved them into his bag without inspection.

"How do we know there will be no searching of the bags?" Astrid posed.

Carolus knelt down, wiped excess blood from the floor. He checked to make sure the shades were still drawn.

"Look as normal as possible." He inspected the pair across from him. They were anything but inconspicuous. Astrid's tired gray eyes sank into her face. Her short and wavy peppered hair sprouted out from her fur hat. The flaps covered her ears like two balled-up squirrels. Delia looked as if she'd just walked off a Fellini set, with a long sequined dress and mink shawl covering her bony shoulders. It was impossible not to stare at the sliver of exposed skin at her neck. "Where are we going in case we get split up?"

Astrid handed him a business card that read:

Poseable Religious Emporium
Karlova 8
Praha 1 - Staré Mesto
110 00

"Very accurate name," Carolus said.

"I see no point in beating bushes."

Delia tugged on her skirt. It had ridden up. It was always the beautiful women who corrected things like that.

CHAPTER 10

December 17
Askasleikir: Bowl Licker

When they arrived in Prague's central terminal, Carolus reveled in the gothic skeleton of the old station. His vision had worsened overnight, and the world became a black-and-white film. The gray goddesses he saw now were as real as he could have ever hoped, and the crystalline sunrise and snow poured into the station from the open rooftop.

Two bronze nymph sculptures, male and female, guarded the exit. Between them was a plaque that read, Praga Mater Urbium. The mother of cities. The cylindrical building made Carolus feel dizzy and weak. Above every spire lay a clock, reminding him that he shouldn't even have been in Prague. This was never part of the plan.

Delia looked frightened to be harboring a man's head in her carry-on. Her eyes glowed misty pink. It was one of the only colors he could still distinguish. He liked seeing her scared; there was something attractive about her helplessness. He knew he shouldn't feel that way, the same way he knew he shouldn't unzip Cass's dress but did it anyway.

Outside, the snow etched great white shadows, veiled and bent against the circular buildings. Carolus had a sick feeling that all the relics of his past had burned in the fire at Hallgrim. He imagined God still smoldering with the remains of the church, clove incense, and flame.

The ancient tracks ran over and through one another like fishing wires. The snow in Prague wasn't like the snow in Reykjavik. It was plusher and more radiant, but it lacked mythology in its joints. In Prague, Carolus couldn't see through to the stars or into the stony eyes of Norse Gods. Prague's was a regal snow, only centuries old.

Astrid hailed a cab and once inside, Carolus pressed his nose against the window as he watched the city scroll by. The small hills and ferns in the distance lit up ivory. Crooked cemeteries reminded him of the days when, by candlelight, he and Cass would visit the gravestones of Vikings they believed had either raised or raped their ancestors. Carolus and Cass's blood and the blood of history were inexorably tangled.

He admired the way the architecture contorted the city and enjoyed the bird-like movements of the small, wooden figures that emerged from clock towers when the hour struck.

* * *

While sitting in the back of the cab, Carolus felt a sudden, violent urge to call Cass; it was as if he felt her presence growing faint. He remembered sitting on the top step of the house while waiting for his mother to wake up on Christmas morning. He knew never to enter her room while she was asleep. It smelled of unwashed gums and peppermint. She once told him that watching a woman sleep is the closest thing to rape—that it was at once intimate and sadistic. He watched Cass though sometimes.

When he clicked shut Cass's door that night and returned to his room, Carolus found Bowl Licker lying in his bed.

"This feels like sleeping on a bunch of dead infants."

"Yeah, well, we can't afford a new one," Carolus said. "Now let me go to sleep."

"You have a long night ahead of you," Bowl Licker announced. His hairy belly slopped over his yellow waistband and jiggled beneath his blue frock. His dirty, pointy feet rested on the sheets. He smelled of beef broth.

"You're going to learn disguise, surveillance. It's about manipulation. You find out about people, learn their routines, fears, and fetishes, and then you exploit them."

"What if they catch me watching?"

"It won't be you they catch. They'll never see you. Besides, buddy boy, voyeurism is often a two-way street—people want you to know about them. They're desperate to be greater than their own small circle of influence. The way they dress is how they want to be perceived. Recurring topics of conversation are what they want to be known for—what they eat, how they fuck. It's all designed for strangers."

That night, young Carolus wore his first wig. His subject was a French girl who moved in down the street. He watched her carefully with more than professional interest. He watched her undress, touching herself under the covers in the fresh air by the window. He imagined that she thought of him, that she knew all along of his presence. After studying her for long enough, he asked her to a music show, and later they made love as if they'd known each other for years. Afterward, they never saw each other again.

By morning, and without warning, Bowl Licker disappeared and Carolus was left alone to watch the last embers of a fire that should have extinguished hours before.

"You saw him again this year?" sixteen-year-old Cass had asked, sitting then at the top step, awake, maybe because she felt Carolus was.

"He hasn't got anyone," Carolus said, lying, hiding the devious behavior he'd learned. He had started lying to his sister.

"Most people don't," she said. "Besides, he's just a Yule Lad."

Cass never felt as close to the Lads as Carolus did; she never found them tragic or terrifying as they passed through the night each Christmas season. The thirteen Yule Lads ranged from mere troublemakers to the homicidal witch, Gryla, and her black cat. Cass never paid them much mind, not even in childhood when they made themselves more available.

He missed Cass now. As the car grumbled along the cobblestone, he tallied all the mistakes he'd ever made. This trip was probably one, but Delia was perdition. And he liked it.

During the ride over, he surreptitiously texted Cass, though he knew he shouldn't.

> Carolus: *Miss your face*
> Cass: *Don't be weird*
> Carolus: *In Prague*
> Cass: *Detour?*
> Carolus: *Definitely*
> Cass: *A girl?*
> Carolus: *Of course.*
> Cass: *Couldn't you have done that here?*
> Carolus: *It's snowing*
> Cass: *Nothing but rain here. Bjorn says hi.*

Carolus: He does not
Cass: I told him you say hi too.
Carolus: I do not
Cass: Safe sex, brother. Don't want any more of you.
Carolus: Do too.

The Poseable Religious Emporium turned out to be much more massive than Carolus imagined and was completely out of place in the fantastic spires and buttresses of Prague's elegant buildings. One giant red smokestack towered above the factory, releasing puffs of white breath. The building was dilapidated: ravaged by ivy, windows cracked or missing. Stucco scabs dimpled its body.

The inside was even more disheveled. It seemed that nothing of any worth could be made in this place—all cement, with bright fluorescent bulbs surrounding the centered skylight. Someone had graffitied all along the walls—dancing bears and coffee cups and penises with bowler hats. Gaping holes in the floor peeked down into a watery basement that reeked of mold. Metal bins like caskets lay about the room, which seemed endless as Carolus followed Astrid and Delia down its belly.

"What do you think of my place of business?" Astrid asked.

"It's a real shit stain," Carolus chimed.

Astrid checked with Delia to make sure her English was correct.

"A shit stain, you say? This is a word not used to describe an empire."

"Like the Japanese?" Carolus dropped his bag in a pile of dust on the right side of the room next to an old conveyor belt that looked as if it hadn't been used in years. He stretched out his aching back. "This machinery is old and rusted."

"I am woman of the earth. The Japanese are of the open waters," Astrid said.

Carolus waited to see if she was kidding, but she wasn't. Delia's eyes wandered and she fidgeted with her earrings. Carolus couldn't believe a woman like her would put up with a place like this. In all of the small corners, gnats the size of pinheads congregated and bred, releasing faint abdominal screams. Carolus found their fornication disturbing.

Delia decided to undress in the main room. Maybe there *were* no other rooms, Carolus thought, just dumpsters and putrid lakes. Astrid attempted to shield Delia with her misshapen body. "My wife, she is unashamed. I have believed that shame is necessary to survival."

"Survival," Delia began, snapping off her stockings, "is the last instinct before death. I have no interest in it."

Astrid turned halfway toward her, running her hands down Delia's wide hips.

"Do you have somewhere to bury those suitcases?" Carolus asked.

"I was in the hope that *you* would," Astrid ventured.

Carolus looked around him as colors dripped out of his vision. He observed a series of upturned factory bins, which looked like metal coffins, that harbored a pile of figures modeled after St. Francis.

Carolus was in another country, off mission. He could just take off. What could they say? He sweated with frustration.

"What's to stop me from leaving you here with the Arab?" he said, annoyed and cold. He had to get to Istanbul and find out who this "brother" was, despite owing Astrid for saving his life. Then again, Astrid had knocked him out in the first place.

Delia ignored them and slipped on a short dress that was probably blue. She emerged from behind Astrid's silhouette, perhaps knowing her presence would calm the situation.

"I was under the thought we would become friends," Astrid said.

Delia walked closer, clicking her fingernails along the piles of Jesuses.

"Have words with our friend," Astrid said to Delia.

Delia took Carolus by the arm. At first he resisted, staring Astrid down, then he let her guide him into the restroom—where she could have changed, he realized. Astrid watched the door swing closed.

"You want to fuck me? Is that it? Then you'll help?" She grabbed his throat and dug her long red nails in, skimming the razor cut. He stood with his hands by his side. "Not a man anymore? Can't defend yourself?" She had something in her mouth, but Carolus couldn't tell what it was.

"I don't hurt women. Keep digging," he said. It was true. The only job he hadn't completed involved a woman. The contract called for a death by houseplant. Apparently, his client's mistress wasn't happy that he'd returned to his wife who lived in the house with the Ficus she'd bought.

Carolus entered the mark's home and knocked him over the head with the pot. It shattered over his skull, but he was still breathing, so Carolus started jamming the roots down his throat. He was about to suffocate when the wife walked in. She was supposed to be off on some Orthodox retreat, but there she was. She didn't hesitate, just threw herself on her husband and began digging the clumps of soil out of his wind-pipe, ignoring Carolus, who was on his knees next to them holding the wet Ficus. There was something very moving about her lack of fear. He admired that. Before she could look up, he darted out the back entrance.

A few days later, he shot the husband point blank in the back of the skull. He gave the client a 30 percent discount because the job hadn't been executed to her specifications.

The black-and-white bathroom tiles glowed in the fluorescent light, and Delia licked her lips. Whatever she'd been biting down on was gone.

"I'm sorry I hurt you," she said, slipping her thumbs under her shoul-der straps and sliding off the non-blue garment. "You have very sad eyes, but I enjoy them." She had nothing underneath the dress, and her curly pubic hair surprised Carolus—it was thick and black like a virgin's.

She was nearly naked and perfect, flawless.

"Talk your way into me," Delia said.

Carolus took off his shirt. "At one point," he started, "I was a cham-pion of table tennis and president of the Icelandic Long-shore Fisher-man's Club."

"You really know how to get a girl going," she teased.

"It's my gift," he said, pulling off his black socks. He liked stepping on the cold tile with his bare feet. There were two curlicue hairs by his big toe.

"This was not in the plans."

Carolus eased next to her warm body on the toilet. "I was thinking the exact opposite."

Slowly, she allowed him past her thighs. Carolus eased deep inside her. He did so carefully and deliberately until she chirped and shook the stalls. He covered her mouth, put his lips against her ear. "You feel like home."

She closed her eyes and let her head loll back. They worked their hips into a rhythm and her body relaxed into his as if accepting him.

Carolus thought of the poseable Jesus and the color of blood. Her eyes were darkened even more in the fluorescent light as he inhaled ammonia. Delia was everything he knew he couldn't avoid. He'd left Reykjavik to escape attachment, and yet, here she was.

CHAPTER 11

December 18
Hurðaskellir: Door Slammer

Carolus woke on the cold bathroom tile and sniffed urine on his sweaty body.

"Was I asleep?" He figured they'd spent a good part of the night in that filthy bathroom and that it was now dawn. In fact, he had only drifted off for an hour, and it was just past midnight. He could tell by the unnatural light filtering through the meter-wide window.

Delia stood over him. "So, you will get rid of that head now?"

"This was business." He said it hoping she would at least deny what he already knew.

She lowered her head, tamping her bare toes on the floor. "No. But it was supposed to be. There will be consequences."

His hands smelled like her, and it was pleasing. This hadn't always been the case—sniffing his fingernails, walking down Laugavegur, the tourists against the hail carrying their hangovers in their bellies like bloated urchins. Who came to Iceland in the winter, anyway? Tourists named Jersey and Tex.

Carolus dressed. He and Delia kissed sweetly but walked out separately. He picked up the two suitcases. "I'll take care of this. Don't worry."

Astrid sat in the exact same spot they'd left her. She observed the two of them, nearly waving, a vacant look in her eyes, as if seeing a ship off at port. She must have been staring at that bathroom door the entire time. Carolus pitied Astrid. She looked ragged.

Carolus left the compound with little idea of how to dispose of the bags. Outside, the wind blustered hard and caught him on the mouth and chin.

He found a red payphone and called Samsa collect, not wanting to use his cell for business.

"In Istanbul?" Samsa questioned, foregoing pleasantries. "My phone bill is coming out of your end."

"In Prague," Carolus answered.

"What have you done?"

"Have I ever gotten us into trouble?"

"Jesus, yes. How many dead?"

"Only one."

"You fuck and drink too much."

"I haven't been drinking," Carolus said.

"Well thank the fucking Christ. What is it that you need? There is an episode of *Kardashians* coming on."

"I need to get rid of some spare auto parts. Know any takers?"

"In Prague? Mother of Jesus. Yes, there's someone. Just don't burn any churches there. They're very old. And keep up on your timetable."

"Hey," he said, looking out at the gray children and the charcoal steeples and faces. "You ever heard of someone losing his sense of color?"

"Like in a movie?"

"No, in life."

"I knew a girl named Katinka who had that effect on men, but I think she's out of the business now."

"Just give me the contact."

When Carolus got out of the taxi, he raced straight to the trunk, not allowing the cabbie to handle his bags. He tipped well and banged on the cottage's front door with his elbow. The man who answered was tall with whiskers instead of a beard—gray-faced, though Carolus knew everyone now appeared in one shade of gray or another. His eyes reminded Carolus of the bloodshot, yellowing ones of Door Slammer as he passed from his mother's room to his own. Footsteps creaked the hinges and woke everyone in the house. He was a foul-mouthed ass whom even Carolus did not like. Often, they'd whisper insults to each other as he passed through the night: "Mollusk." "Pansy." "Two-assed llama."

Carolus's mind returned to his youth to a particular December 18— the night before his mother's wake, when Door Slammer kept him up by thumping his bedroom door every time he was about to doze off.

***

"I don't want to be sick like you all," Carolus had yelled, pulling the covers over his nose. He felt unclean. His mother wouldn't approve of the way he'd made his money. He knew he was becoming someone she wouldn't recognize. He could've gone to college like Cass if he hadn't tended to his mother, paid her bills. He didn't regret it, though. He'd already worked a few jobs for Samsa by then. The money was good, but he hadn't liked the results. It wasn't like stabbing rabbits in the woods.

"Do you know why we help you?" Slammer asked, kneeling at Carolus's bed. "Because you're one of us now, you insolent lima bean."

"You're just making me into a goddamn monster." Carolus's nightmares of death had started with the horrific memories of early kills. Kills he'd botched. Watching them bleed out in long, slow gasps. He felt consumed by their bodies and his mother's body. She was the only person he'd ever really wanted to save. Her disease was far more violent than anything Carolus could ever enact.

"You can take care of your sister just like your mother would want. But you've got to take your lessons," Slammer said. "Just be a good lad and take your teaching."

Carolus rolled off the covers, pulled on his boots, and grabbed his bowie knife. During his mother's service the next morning, he could hardly keep his eyes open, drifting in and out of darkness.

***

Snow covered the lawn in front of his contact's house. It obscured the birdbath and tall bushes that blocked the neighbors' views. The house looked like it had been whittled from a single tree—all wooden exterior with twelve finely-carved pink poles separating the first tier of the house from the porch. Above that, more poles supported a steeple with one window. Up and up it went until there was a tiny gazebo on top that had a view of the rest of the neighborhood like a dungeon tower. The house was a custard color, though Carolus saw it as a shade of green. Someone had drawn curtains in front of all eight windows.

The man at the front door did not extend his gloved hand. "My name is Bedrich. I was told you have a muffler to dispose of," he said. This was common jargon. No one liked to come right out and say they were dealing in body parts.

Carolus lifted the two bags. Bedrich got out of his way. Carolus never liked cleanup men. Always dangerous and rat-like, he thought; they often smelled of cabbage and at any moment might pass gas without so much as altering their posture.

Bedrich had decorated the room as if it were a Roman villa: with fountains and metal grapes. He'd hung tapestries of all kinds of circus acts and orgies on the wall. Drapes hung down around the hallways like something out of *The Great Gatsby*. A male servant came to take away the bags, but Carolus held onto them tightly.

"Don't worry. He is a trusted advisor of mine," Bedrich assured him.

"I'm used to working alone," Carolus said.

"Then what are you doing here?"

"Cleaning up other people's shit."

"Now you sound like me."

"Hey," Carolus said, feeling like he should leave. "You ever lose your sense of color?"

"Woman problems?"

"Maybe."

Bedrich lifted the bags and opened the door to his basement with his foot. "Want to watch?"

Carolus thought of the other time he'd heard that phrase—a man in Húsavík had wanted to watch his wife get fucked good for once. "Proper fucked," Carolus recalled. When had his mind become so warped that he would consider this proposition?

The servant returned, held open the door. "This way," he said to Carolus. "You really should watch Mr. Bedrich work."

Carolus wondered if he had anywhere to sleep. He should at least let Astrid cool off. The train could wait, he thought. He wanted to see Delia again.

Istanbul seemed so far away. His mark felt further from him now than ever before. Perhaps this journey might transform him into someone whole. He could never have wished himself on anyone.

Carolus followed the servant down into the basement. He had now crossed every line in his profession; he might as well break another, he thought. "Any whisky?" he asked, and the servant shoved a glass in his hand as if he'd already inquired.

The basement was a perfect rectangle with only a plastic bathtub and a series of metal poles in the middle of the hardwood floor. Posters of Gretta Garbo and Harpo Marx clung to the walls. There were no windows, and the space reeked of bleach. Bedrich opened the bags. Carolus closed his eyes as he sipped the whisky, but it didn't cover the stench of human decay and cologne.

Bedrich picked up the Arab's head. Carolus had forgotten to shut his remaining eyelid, which was bad form under any circumstances.

"How did he die?" Bedrich asked.

Carolus tipped back his glass so that the ice collected on his top lip. "Stabbed with a Jesus."

Bedrich made the sign of the cross with his index finger. "Everyone has his beliefs."

The servant immediately refilled the glass. Whatever he was filling it with was good. It stuck to Carolus's guts like real whisky does and burned. It had been a while since Carolus allowed himself a drink, and it felt good in his empty stomach.

Bedrich dug into the larger suitcase and pulled out bloody parts from the plastic lining. A leg, then a torso. It reminded Carolus of a potato he'd assembled into a man when he was younger. The dead man had the same raisin eyes.

With the help of his servant, who may well have also been his lover, Bedrich began to reconstruct the Arab in the bathtub. It was gruesome, but required creativity and a twisted sense of duty that Carolus found admirable. He'd probably begun by dismembering and plucking the beaks and wings off of birds, creating entirely new species: robins with blue breasts and long beaks. Maybe it felt good to make someone decent before desecrating his remains.

Bedrich twisted the Arab's head onto his ribcage and straightened his tie through the blood. He didn't even wear goggles, which made Carolus think he was a little sick and careless.

"Do you want to save anything?" the servant asked.

"No," Bedrich said.

The servant poured lye on the body from the head down. It burned Carolus's nostrils. The man's hair dripped onto his crotch and burned its way through his legs. Bedrich turned on "Stuck In the Middle With You" and pulled a long shaving razor from his jacket pocket.

"Like the *Reservoir Dogs*," he said and lopped off the Arab's ear, already soft and putty-like from the lye. "You know? Quentin?"

The lye created gaping, festering holes in the body. Carolus watched the Arab burn away as if he'd never existed.

"You know this, Tarantino?"

"Yes!" Carolus exclaimed finally. "I know the movie."

"Oh, good," Bedrich continued.

Carolus gulped down his whisky, but this time the servant was not there to refill it. He sloshed the ice around in circles. The cubes clinked at the bottom of the glass, just beyond the music.

"Don't you like American movies?" Bedrich asked. He motioned to the servant to switch off the song. "Tarantino, he comes in the winters to your country. I feel he and I would have much in common."

Carolus nodded skeptically. "I like your house. It's unusual."

"You appreciate the eccentric. My former lover, he used to tell me in bed, 'You're the strangest man I've ever been inside of.'"

Carolus thought of all the strange women he'd been inside of—the biters and the chokers, the bound, the daddy's girls, the spankers, slappers, and nipple twisters. He thought of Delia and how she wasn't any of that, but she wasn't good either. She was like him: indefinable. He wondered what Cass would say if she knew of his sexual past. If she'd love him the same way.

"Got more whisky?" Carolus asked. He pulled a smoke from his shirt pocket, crumpled and leaking tobacco. As he lit up, he noticed the servant scrubbing the walls of the tub. The sides were caked with bits of knuckle hair and polyester.

Bedrich poured him another drink. "I wouldn't take you for a drinker."

"Then you don't know Iceland."

"I don't," he confirmed.

"We had a beer ban until '89. You know that?" Carolus couldn't fathom what it would have been like to live in the era of prohibition. He imagined the Yule Lads cooking pots of poison and pawning it off as gin. What puritanical messes the damning few create.

"I don't," Bedrich said.

"You ever feel like you're enjoying your job too much?"

Bedrich started up the stairs, so Carolus followed, waiting for an answer. It was much brighter in the living room, and his eyes adjusted slowly to the sparrow and flower wallpaper and the swirling Tuscan rugs. The house extended further back, but Carolus had no intentions of prying.

"I don't like killing. But I enjoy the aftermath. It's submissive. I like to create with the remains. I like to improve," Bedrich answered.

"You ever travel for your work?"

"It's not only the Czechs who get themselves into trouble, of course. I charge traveling fees. My assistant accompanies me for his various services." Bedrich handed Carolus a napkin with a number on it. "A man in your profession may need simple hands like mine."

"I'll keep that in mind," Carolus said. He finished his whisky, handed Bedrich an envelope full of cash, and left.

On the ride back to the emporium, Carolus recalled the vision of Delia's curvy body against the lines of the tile. Out of the cab window, he noticed green in the gray and black that swept through the streets. It was a short ride, and the door to the emporium was curiously ajar when he arrived. Inside, the factory was dark.

CHAPTER 12

Carolus pushed open the emporium door. Without the lights on, great white beams from the moon shone through the dusty windows. Seven distinct portals illuminated the factory floor, which Carolus realized was now ankle-high and bumpy. He walked further inside. Someone had overturned the oak bins and metal canisters that restrained the figurines. Various religious figures, the likes of Gandhi and Zoroaster, lay at his feet—tossed and broken, forming a sacred carpet of plastic. It felt unholy and satisfying to step on the torso of Martin Luther and the neck of Confucius.

He hadn't looked up before, but a crossword of thick red beams ran across the factory ceiling. There was something dynamic in their asymmetry. He imagined them in many colors and wished he could smell like Delia again instead of reeking of lye and whisky.

A trail of blood ran along the floor all the way to the back door. As Carolus approached the area of the spilled Jesuses, he tasted Delia. He shouldn't have left her alone, he thought. He should've protected her. He tried to convince himself it was impossible to love someone he hardly knew, someone who wasn't even his to love. He tried to remember what the Lads had said about the pitfalls of attachment, and how once, during a school play, he'd fallen in love and had his heart broken between the second and third acts. It made his ankles feel weak. Carolus sat down in a pile of Billy Grahams.

His mother would sometimes sit him down and explain to him that a woman's body was like an old shirt. She never said why it was that way; when he asked, she'd tell him that he had a lot to learn about women and that a man is responsible for the heart of his lover, the heart of his next lover, and least of all his own. Maybe she was a feminist, but more likely, she'd just been hurt by bodybuilding Icelandic men and their tiny brains and hearts.

He let his hands drift over the crude plastic, bending arms and legs, twisting their heads right and left at his whim. All of their muscles raised, veiny and distorted. It was hard to see the blood in the cloud-covered moonlight, but there was a struggle-induced thickness to it. He knew blood the way a vintner knows grapes.

The line of blood led straight to the pile of Jesuses. Maybe someone was trying to send a message. And then he saw Delia's hand—motionless and only slightly visible under the mountains of action figures. He could tell from her mint nail polish. There was nothing Carolus hated more than finding a young woman's corpse. He immediately regretted sleeping with her because of the pain it had caused both of them.

Carolus slowly walked over. He should leave, he thought. He should get out and never see her this way, but he needed to get one final look. He knelt down, his knee cold and aching on the cement floor. He grabbed her hand and tugged her body upward. He hated that all he really wanted was what remained of her. He wanted to carry her with him and feel her cold breath against his neck for the rest of his life.

"Be gentle!" Delia whispered.

"Jesus, fuck! I thought you were dead." Carolus staggered backward, tripping over figurines. He held his chest dramatically. Delia looked very pale but beautiful. She resembled an American cowgirl, dressed in jeans and a white T-shirt. He'd always been attracted to cowgirls ever since he saw an American football game on satellite television and became infatuated with a Detroit cheerleader. Carolus felt a great relief in his belly, followed by shame because he wanted her dead or alive. He wanted every part of her to be his.

"I didn't know who it was, so I hid." She stood up, kicked away the Jesuses, and lit a cigarette. She shook, and Carolus placed his warm hands on her shoulders. It steadied her, and her eyes softened, something shaking in them, perhaps a memory, before she glanced away.

"Where's Astrid?"

"They took her. She pleaded for my life and they left me, eventually."

"Who?"

"They said they were looking for you," Delia exhaled the words with smoke. She didn't have a scratch on her.

"They asked for me by name?"

"They said, 'Where's the perverted Icelandic motherfucker?'"

"Fair enough. Whose blood is that?" He pointed to the long trail by the exit.

She looked over. "When they tried to grab me . . ."

Carolus followed the clotting blood pools. "It must've been pretty bad."

She held up her long green nails. For the moment, the story didn't matter to Carolus. He wasn't accustomed to having people he cared about brought back to life. He wished they could make love right there on the figurines.

"You'll have to bring me with you if you want to do that," Delia said, tossing her lit cigarette in the figurine pile.

"Do what?" Carolus wondered now if he hadn't only lost his sense of color. Had he spoken out loud?

"I've been a woman long enough to know that look. That's fine, but you're taking me with you to Istanbul. You can have me all you want along the way."

Carolus closed the distance between them and gently grasped her chin. He sniffed her cherry-scented breath. "I don't usually take women where I'm going."

"You stink of whisky."

"You're nagging me already? We haven't left yet."

"Drink until you're limp. No skin off me. Just get us back to Astrid."

"We'd better head for the station," Carolus said. He looked up at the snaking pipelines and scaffolding overhead. He remembered the Arab's open eye like a keyhole.

CHAPTER 13

December 19
Skyrgámur: Skyr Gobbler

> SKYR:
> Kyr = *þéttir* (if not available, use 1 tbsp. live culture sour cream
>   or buttermilk)
> Rennet
> Skim milk

Carolus dreamt that he had covered his genitals and eyes in Skyr and was bathing in his mother's tub with Cass. He liked the taste of Skyr because it was actually fresh cheese, not yogurt like everyone thought, and they only made it in Iceland. He couldn't see Cass, but he smelled her—her and the Skyr.

Slowly, the Skyr began to dissipate from his crotch, and he formed an erection. He wiped the cheese from his eyes, looked at the figure across from him in the tub, and screamed. It wasn't Cass. It was Skyrgamur, the fattest Lad. The folds of his rippling belly sucked in the Skyr, lingering on its long black hairs. He'd gotten the cream all over his face, and his blond hair reached down over his black eyes so that he couldn't even witness his own shame. Skyrgamur had been licking his genitals for the sweet cheese, and now they stared at each other like old and broken lovers, warm and aroused in a tub of animal product and fingernail dirt.

Carolus awoke to Delia's hand slapping him across the face.

"What's the matter with you?" he bellowed.

"You were screaming, but you had a hard-on, so I wasn't sure if I should wake you or not."

Carolus looked around. The train vibrated along the track, and he heard his luggage rattling above him. "I had a dream about Skyr."

"Is that a woman?" Delia asked.

She'd already applied her makeup and looked prepared for an adventure. She'd shut the window shades, but Carolus figured it must have been morning. It felt like morning. "It's a fresh cheese yogurt only made in Iceland."

"Sounds disgusting," she said.

"When I was a kid, we'd fight over the last blueberry pack, and sometimes there'd be a prize like a sheep whistle or skin cream."

"It's strange to be traveling without Astrid. I think I like the feeling."

"Where are we?" Carolus asked. He raised the shade. The scenery had turned mostly to hat factories and wine country. A pale morning sun. He'd have to arrive in Istanbul by the twenty-fourth to perform this job to his standards.

"I think we're somewhere in Hungary." She climbed over and straddled him, distractedly searching out the window. Her knees dug into his thighs and her breasts pressed against his head, but it was all very pragmatic somehow, as she strained to take in the cool air from the open window.

"You know, I always wondered why women close their eyes during sex." Carolus tried to shift his head uncomfortably.

"Because that's what they do in the movies," Delia said. "In the cinema, if you have your eyes open, you're thinking about something else."

"I guess that's true." Carolus ran his fingernail over his dry lips. It smelled like smoke.

"Did you have your eyes open?"

"I don't remember."

Delia ran her hand through Carolus's hair, returning her gaze to him. Her pupils appeared silvery red. "You could use a cut," she said.

His hair had been a little wild before he left, and he hadn't looked in a mirror for a couple of days. He needed a shower and a smoke. He worried about Cass. This was the longest they'd been apart since right after the funeral when he took a job in Monaco. He imagined the terrible conversations between her and Bjorn:

"Look, honey, aren't my pants fine and expertly pressed?"

"I wonder where Carolus is. I miss him. He should be home for Christmas like always."

"Look at the sheep I've slaughtered. Aren't they fine and expertly pressed?"

Carolus believed Bjorn likely slaughtered defenseless farm animals in his free time. Only a man with something to hide works with soaps. Not that he didn't have secrets of his own. But if his mother were alive, she never would have allowed Cass to marry such a dial tone.

Carolus remembered laying under the Christmas tree, looking through the white lights. The scent of evergreen poured over them. His mother had ornamented her hair with gold and teal ribbons that were meant for the presents—always socks or small French currency she'd found by the sea. To him, she was very beautiful.

"Could you get me some coffee?" Delia asked.

He nodded, and she rolled off of him. He got up and wandered through the train into the Manor car in search of coffee when he suddenly found himself alone and surrounded by parrots—all one form of gray or another. There were also marmots, cats, and iguanas.

He lit up a cigarette. He'd never much liked parrots. He felt more akin to mountain beasts—those who could survive desolation.

"No smoking in here," a voice called out. It was unusually deep for a parrot, Carolus thought, but the voice repeated itself. "No smoking in here."

"Fuck you, parrot," he said.

"Fuck you," the parrot repeated.

Carolus eyed each parrot in the room, looking for the culprit. "Who the fuck takes a parrot on a train, anyway?"

"Where are you going?"

He took a long drag of his cigarette and flicked it near the cages. The birds flapped their wings and squawked. "You like that, you fucking parrot?"

"You're a parrot."

"You're the parrot!" Carolus blurted. He headed for the exit. Something latched onto his shoulder.

The same voice boomed, "Mr. Grumson says 'Hello.'" Who the fuck was Grumson? He had no time to think it over, as two men descended on him. Carolus could only throw one good punch at the man to his left before he was knocked unconscious again by Thomas Grumson's second-place football trophy.

CHAPTER 14

Carolus awoke in a Volkswagen Jetta. It smelled like a rental car—pine and leather cleaner. A gnat wrestled against the windows, forming polka dots on breath condensation. Two men sat in the front seats. They'd devised a makeshift divider out of a piece of bus stop Plexiglas with a mesh rectangular hole in the center. Carolus looked down at his slacks and noticed a lot of blood. The seatbacks were gray, but a German gray. The sky was overcast, but a little blue peeked through the clouds. His fingertips seemed peach or human beige. He'd gotten most of it back. He'd never truly appreciated color until that moment. He wondered if Delia was all right.

"So, where are you taking me in this college girl hatchback?" Carolus questioned.

"It is not a hatchback," the driver said. "It gets excellent mileage."

"Don't tell him that," the passenger said.

"Do you have a destination?" Carolus asked.

"We are taking you to Mr. Grumson. We made that clear when we hit you, but perhaps we sabotaged your memory during the battle."

"It wasn't much of a battle. I thought you were a parrot."

"Yes, well, precautions were taken," the driver admitted.

"Your imitation was excellent," Carolus said.

"Your Icelandic wit will not persuade us to release you." The driver rolled down his window and spat. Saliva leaked down the window and onto the car.

"Do you want a tissue?" the passenger asked.

"Do not ask me this again," the driver said. "I don't use tissues."

The driver had blond hair and broad shoulders. A mole jiggled on his neck just above his lime-colored polyester suit. The passenger had big ears and dark hair. He wore a much nicer black pea coat.

Carolus lay across the seat. His head wound dripped onto the leather. "You didn't happen to bring my bag, did you?"

Neither spoke.

"I liked you better when you were parrots," he said.

"We were never actually parrots," the driver reminded him.

"Well said. You don't have any food do you?"

"Under the seat," the passenger replied.

He reached down to find two sandwiches. If they'd thought to bring him food, Carolus thought, they weren't about to kill him. Not yet, anyway.

CHAPTER 15

Carolus was at home with Cass, the dog on his lap licking his knee. He knew it was a dream, but it was comfortable and warm.

"I missed you," he said.

"Everyone asked about you at Christmas. The Doorway Sniffer even came by to wish you well. He smelled my armpits."

"He's a good man."

"They're not men," Cass disputed.

Carolus understood then that he and his sister were very different, even in dreams. These Yule Lads were sad souls, but they taught him his trade. Back home he was important. Back home, they could confide in him—move from rock to rock under his guidance. Together they'd sniff lace bread from miles away and chase the steamy scent all the way to the ocean, all the way to the ice and Mrs. Snorrason's house where she baked unceasingly until Christmas Day. Maybe she was afraid she would not live to see it.

Carolus wanted to move toward his sister, but the dog wouldn't leave, so he sat motionless on the couch as she opened the door. Bjorn arrived with an armful of soaps. Carolus threw off the dog and slapped Bjorn across the face. Cass cried. He took a hatchet and cut off Bjorn's soapy hands. Cass threw her body on Bjorn and begged.

"I'll do anything, Carolus. Leave him be. I'll do anything. I'll do anything you want," she pleaded, desperation in her voice.

Carolus woke in the back of the Volkswagen. Outside, a hard rain fell, and black horses ran alongside the car.

His captors stopped along the highway at a Dutch saloon. They brought Carolus with them.

The driver showed Carolus his gun. "Don't play stupid, and we can eat casually. We clear?"

"That was all very clear," Carolus said.

The passenger followed behind.

Inside, a woman tended bar, surrounded mostly by brass and wooden shelving that kept jugs, not bottles, of nameless alcohol. A few patrons sat away from the bar toward the back. Carolus felt like he was in a Clint Eastwood movie.

"Three Absinthes," the driver said. "They got the good stuff here. The old stuff they don't make anymore."

The driver and passenger sat on either side of him at wooden bar stools. He got a good look at their faces. Neither had any interesting scars or skin grafts. That was probably why they hadn't been caught yet. Two grim individuals: murderers no doubt. Yet, they had the potential to be decent company. The driver's mustache looked as if it might scab off any second. The passenger's eyes were too close together—like someone trying to see his own nose.

They downed shots of flaming Absinthe. The hot licorice flavor burned Carolus's throat. He ogled the bartender's breasts and began to pick apart her most engrossing features, pairing them with the legs and eyelashes and thighs of other women. "She's an odd-looking one, isn't she?"

The driver looked straight at her. "She really is."

"I can hear you," she said.

"Then get us another round," the passenger retorted.

These were his kind of men, Carolus thought.

"Try this," Carolus said. With his fingers in the air, he cupped the image of her breasts and placed them on the woman sitting in the booth next to the door.

The driver and the passenger downed their Absinthe. "That's a real beautiful trick," the passenger said. Fugue drunk, he took the woman's eyes and tossed them to the ground, then he snatched the pea green eyes of a girl mopping the floor by the jukebox. He took her ass, too. Now they were getting somewhere, Carolus thought.

Carolus drew with his fingers along the line of the light, rearranged the face so it wasn't glowering. He downed another round of Absinthe. His mother had told him that women required love exactly as God had made them, no matter how poodle-faced. Carolus never had trouble loving women's flaws, sweet inconsistencies from nature. He found them all equally acceptable, but he never imagined having the ability to craft in this way—picking and choosing the body and the mind. He felt limitless power that God must have felt in his groin on the seventh day—that great, furious build-up of creation that led, inevitably, to Eve.

The driver plucked the eyebrows of a girl he said he'd dated in college and placed them on the fantastic figure they'd formed. They grabbed behind the bar for more Absinthe, swigged it back. The bar maid screamed.

"Stop, lady," Carolus begged. "If you stop, they won't hurt you." Green booze dribbled down his mouth. He could feel the intoxication: light and titillating. Not like whisky, which was heavy and leathery. The passenger and driver each snatched their own bottles. "I don't even know your name."

"Aaltie," she said, not at all frightened. Anyway, the men in front of her were murderers, not rapists, and maybe she felt that. Maybe she wasn't afraid to die. Though not many have that gift. It's a good feeling, Carolus remembered. The first time you're ready. Then, one day, it just goes away, and you're terrified as hell. He was frightened now, but the liquor dulled it. It sat sharp in his belly like a knife.

Carolus wobbled in his seat, and a Bjork song came on the box that reminded him of a girl with hair on her nipples whose name he couldn't remember. The image vanished. Carolus wished the girl they'd imagined was out wandering amongst the living.

CHAPTER 16

December 20
Bjúgnakrækir: Sausage Snatcher

Carolus slept through the night in the car as the scenery changed. The landscape became blue-crossed domes that towered over the white adobe buildings overlooking the water. They'd reached Greece. Somehow, he'd come to an understanding with the driver and the passenger.

Carolus enjoyed color in a way he hadn't since he was a boy chasing white wolves and red sleds. He recalled many times over the holidays waking up to find the copper-skinned blood sausage he'd left in the meat drawer was gone. Only the soft sleeves of translucent skin remained. He'd often made the mistake of buying sausage around Christmas because it was cheaper, and he figured the Sausage Snatcher might satiate himself somewhere else one year. He never did.

His mother would scold him for spending the Skyr and butter money on bratwurst and Andouille while knowing it would rest in the belly of that "swine-cunny," as she'd like to call him.

On the way to their destination, Carolus and his kidnappers stopped at many pubs and roadside dives, trying to recreate that first experience, but they never could. Bios, red lit and brooding, Gazaki with its winged women on the walls, and Astron, known for its spectacularly dusty light fixtures. During the journey, they often pissed into the wind and shared prostitutes. They became, for lack of a better word, acquaintances. Men of the same business. Carolus figured there was no point in slipping away. He'd face this thing head-on. That's what he'd always done. That's what the Lads had taught him to do all those years ago.

When they were done with a prostitute, Carolus would take her out for a bite to eat. "Do you enjoy whoring?" he asked, shoveling pancakes into his mouth.

"Yes, it's OK," she said. She had a misshapen mole on her left cheek, which seemed very cliché for a woman in her profession. Her teeth were slightly yellowed and showed too much when she spoke. She dressed modestly, but maybe that was because of the cold, Carolus thought.

"Was I good?" he asked.

"You were very good, mister," she said, flashing her teeth. She'd ordered ham on a baguette and asked for lettuce on the side to place on the sandwich. "For crispness," she said, acknowledging his stare.

Her processed red hair felt like wool on his cheeks. Prostitutes always seemed worn, he thought, like a book that bends too easily. "Do you tell every customer he's good?"

"Men enjoy to hear they're good. Women, bad. I proffer pleasure."

"I'll give you that," he said, guzzling coffee. It was hot and burned the roof of his mouth. The driver and passenger lay upstairs in their beds in the small bed and breakfast. They trusted him, maybe because they knew he could have left anytime. A sign of respect. No doubt they'd looked into his work. He was, after all, a craftsman. The Sausage Snatcher, a butcher by trade, had taught him how to use a blade.

* * *

Snatcher wore a jean jacket and a fedora. They'd hang a butcher's pig on the birch tree in the backyard, and Carolus would hack at it.

"Pig skin is similar to human skin," Snatcher said. "If you can gut a pig, you can gut a guy."

Carolus remembered searching the pig's eyes, wondering if there was a soul inside. It wriggled against the ropes around its hooves, squealing. "Does it have to be alive?" Carolus said.

"All the more incentive to make a clean cut," Snatcher said, handing him the carving knife.

It was never clean the first time.

* * *

That day on the road, the driver sipped a Red Bull and swore at the landscape. He'd drunk too much, and the hangover washed over his face and his lungs. Carolus knew the feeling. The passenger snored, his head flush against the window.

"You guys are all right," Carolus said.

"I am not supposed to be so comfortable with you as I am." The driver rubbed his temples, one hand on the wheel. "Fucking Greeks. All their trees look goddamn the same." A line of square greenery bordered the road.

"The women have big breasts here," Carolus said, eyeing a couple of girls tending to a vineyard in the distance. "Those two have gotta be at least a hundred meters away, and I can make out their nipples. That's amazing."

"You are fond of big nipples?"

"I'm not opposed to them," Carolus said.

"No, I imagine you don't oppose much about women. I oppose women. I oppose them very much."

Carolus breathed deeply. It felt good to taste the tannin in his lungs. He lit a smoke and inhaled that, too. He tried to take as much as he could into his body. He breathed with pleasure. "I've seen you, driver. You like women enough."

"I am no delicate flower, no. But even the good ones use you up. Women, they keep things hidden away."

"No, you're no flower, my friend."

"We are not friends," the driver protested.

In that moment, Carolus realized they would kill him. He'd fooled himself all along into thinking there was some kind of larger plan. But why in Istanbul? Why not knock him off and bury him in the wine fields? Why not in the train when he was unconscious?

Carolus leaned in close, wrapped his arm around the driver's seat through the hole in the divider, which had been left open past nights. He clicked his nails against the dangling seatbelt next to the driver's ear.

"Shhh. I am still within my hangover."

Along the left-hand side, individual ruined columns appeared. He remembered his fourth-year teacher shooshing him like the driver did and how later he realized it sounded just like somebody suffocating. He really didn't enjoy such personal forms of massacre. It was better to push a button, pull a trigger, bait a dog, or pay a vagrant. He remembered their purple and green faces—not clearly like memories, but faint and deconstructed like dreams.

The columns appeared more regularly along the side of the road, pieces of something grander. A few Spanish tourists—he could tell by their hats—meandered around, flashing digital pictures of the rubble.

"Why is it that it's always the loneliest fucking people who shoosh you? It's always the motherfuckers who should be goddamn thrilled to hear a sound other than their fist around their own cock," Carolus huffed.

The driver got nervous and peered over at the sleeping passenger. "Gregory," he said, not taking his hands off the wheel.

"Is that his name? I figured him for a Luscious. You, maybe Dalton. Is it Dalton?"

"Gregory," he said louder. "Maybe you could sit back now."

Carolus inched up, placing his hand on the driver's shoulder through the hole in the divide. "Dalton, friend, are you afraid?"

The driver reached out and clutched Gregory's jacket. Carolus stretched hard to grab the wheel. His face jammed against the divider. Sweat dripped into Carolus's eyes as he struggled to gain control. He thought of his mother struggling to breathe. He took a breath, exhaled. With one hand, he spun the car straight left into a stone column by the roadside. Dalton's body shot through the window on impact, creating a jagged circle in the windshield. His body landed away from the car. Carolus banged forward, cracked the middle console in with his shoulder blade and somehow landed in Gregory's lap. The passenger had been strapped in and now rubbed his stiff neck in shock. Outside, a few stunned Spanish tourists ambled toward the car.

Blood oozed down from a gash on his forehead. Carolus checked his aching jaw then turned up toward Gregory. "Have you made your peace?"

Gregory couldn't move enough to look Carolus in the eyes. "Can't say I have," Gregory said. With his pointer and middle fingers, Carolus pushed Gregory's eyes through his skull—a slow, squirting death.

Carolus rifled around in Gregory's pockets and found a sealed envelope, stuffing it into his coat. He wondered if any of the tourists saw what he did as they crowded around the car, stepping over glass and blood and rock. Carolus figured he should make his peace sometime soon so the same wouldn't happen to him. His mother always told him not to go to bed angry.

He opened up the driver's side door and pushed through the Spaniards. "Está bien?" they asked.

The car had crashed into what had been a temple and dented one of the three pillars left standing. Some structures, he thought, had succumbed to time, war, Christianity. Others were never built to last. The pillars were bright white with birds and men etched into them. The grass around the ruins burned green and brown. Carolus stared into a stone archway for a moment. As he walked past the frightened, gawking Spaniards, he asked, "Whose temple was this?"

The group skulked around the shattered vehicle and made cell phone calls. Some lifted pieces of rubble off the hood and stuffed them into their handbags for souvenirs. A tall, blunt-headed man, maybe a doctor, checked the bodies for pulses—but men like them never had any. Past the archway stood a sculpture. It was a winged phallus with balls that had been worn down over time.

"Dionysus," a Spanish tourist declared.

Carolus had always been fond of the God of wine and sex. He'd been stitched to Zeus's thigh until he was ready to be born, then raised by mountain nymphs, which Carolus felt resembled the Lads, except much more beautiful and without the odor of low tide. His worshipers would reach a maddened state in the woods and rip apart anything they came across. Carolus understood that madness, but he harnessed it—as much as possible, anyway.

How lucky to be placed in the loins of his favorite god, one ripped limb from limb by his own followers in an orgy so intense they couldn't distinguish blood from wine and semen.

Carolus spread his arms out as far as he could, wishing he could reach either end of the thirteen columns that now engulfed him. In the sun, he could make out the purple and mint vegetation that had grown over the puritanical centuries. He wished to tear them away and lick the ground in worship.

Between the columns, the Spanish tourists appeared as a chorus and began to close in on his figure, silhouetted and ridged against the riveted stone flooring. Three women and five men. One with a boy on his shoulders began to curse and yelp in Spanish. Carolus understood that *hijo de puta* meant "motherfucker" and *prostituta punta* meant "toe prostitute." Maybe he was wrong about the second one.

As they came closer, Carolus felt excited and terrified at the idea that he might die in the same way as a sex god. It was the death he'd once craved, but no one, not even a god himself, could truly accept death in the moment it was upon him. He could hear Dionysus scream as his joints stretched and his skin began to rip at the seams. It was a horrifying conclusion to immortality. The group closed in on Carolus, and he braced himself for the pain, shutting his eyes tight.

CHAPTER 17

December 21
Gluggagægir: Window Peeper

As Carolus prepared to be torn apart, he heard a click. He loosened his clenched fists. There was no pain. He heard another click, and he opened his eyes to flashes. Camera flashes. They were photographing him. He ran up to them, grabbed their cameras, and smashed them into bits of yellow and black plastic.

Carolus pushed aside the Spaniards and headed for the driver's body. No sense in leaving him alive, he thought. But the driver was dead. Kneeling next to his head, Carolus noticed a small opening where gnats fought their way through membrane and glass. Carolus couldn't help feeling a sense of unease that he was being targeted by something much larger and more obscene than he'd suspected.

Extricating himself from the crowd, he opened the envelope with his thumb. The paper inside was a letter that read:

> *Congratulations on murdering these thugs. I had no doubts.*
>   *One of them—Gregory, I think—had a child, Julia. Her*
>   *photograph is included.*
> *Don't remember me yet, brother?*
> *What about the Ficus?*
> *I took the liberty of handing the Istanbul police photos of you*
>   *by the hot springs. Happy hunting.*

A small school photograph of a young girl fluttered to the ground. Carolus quickly picked it up and stuffed it into his pocket. He tried not to think about her. Julia. He concentrated on the Ficus. So, a dead man was chasing him. A dead man who knew about his trip to Istanbul. In the distance, sirens wound.

The last thing Carolus could afford was to get caught with a couple of dead hitmen. A dark-skinned woman with short curly hair shielded her children's sight, but young eyes have a way of finding holes through knuckles. They grimly observed the two shattered men leaking death onto the ground alongside rock and glass. Becoming smaller, harder. Many frightened tourists dialed on their cell phones and wailed gorgeous coiling words. With everyone distracted, Carolus commandeered the Buick of a man who was trying to resuscitate the driver. God help him if he does, he thought. The car was running when he got in, so it saved him the trouble of pretending he knew how to jump-start something, which seemed to always work in the movies.

Carolus didn't feel bad about stealing when it was necessary, but he wished he'd taken something more practical. American cars were made for fucking, not driving. As he looked back, the ruins and steam disappearing from his view, he ran one hand over the leather seat of the Buick Skylark. The Skylark was red with a black stripe down its hood—very indiscreet. He poked his head out, letting the cool wind dry his sweaty hair. He hadn't showered in a couple of days, and he smelled like bought sex. Most women smell like eucalyptus or oranges. Prostitutes smell like drugstore cologne and saliva.

* * *

It was the twenty-first of December already; he was behind schedule. He associated the date with Glugg, the Window Peeper, who had taught him true voyeurism. He wasn't as sinister as many believed, Carolus thought. He headed east along E94, somewhere in the direction of Turkey at 177 kilometers per hour, the sirens now dissipating. Glugg was not, foremost, a pervert. He did, however, occasionally transgress. He was unassuming, with thick black Woody Allen glasses and a puffy beard that belied his age: five hundred.

He kept his toenails pedicured, and even on the coldest winter days, he wore thong sandals that smelled like the inside of an owl. His face was still that of a boy's, but his skin had yellowed and his eyes had dulled, making it clear that he'd lived for too long. Still, he had a penchant for voyeurism and petty theft that was admirable in a twisted sort of way—and really, Carolus thought, was a peek at a titty or a missing knee-high anything to sulk over? He might sniff the stocking or rub it, but he never did anything truly sinful. Glugg never acted against God.

"The Window Peeper is a no-good horny sonofabitch," Cass would say. "He's a rapist and a thief."

"That's how rumors spread," Carolus said. He usually knitted or played with his pet lima beans in the icy evenings before Christmas.

"He saw my bush," Cass said.

"You have a bush?" Carolus only later realized that she hadn't meant shrubbery.

"You don't know anything," she hissed and walked into her room, pretending to lock the door. Carolus knew she secretly hoped he'd burst in and plead for her forgiveness. He would play the scenario over and over in his mind: Cass prostrate on her yellow comforter, her eyeliner running in long black gashes like Indian paint. Her bed was a sacred place, softer than any he'd ever know. Probably none of it was true, and she was in there reading Marie Claire.

* * *

When he traveled, Carolus took as many side roads as possible because they, like oak rings, told how ancient something was. The oldest cities bloomed from the inside out: contorting, claustrophobic horse alleys at their center surrounded by swelling circles of industry. Greece tasted different, like Ouzo and fog and the scent of lamb. As a boy, he'd enjoyed licorice much more than Cass had, so he and his mother would split a single candy, licking each piece until it vanished.

It was funny to have traveled so far and to have killed for a job that meant nothing to him. Another paycheck (bigger, of course), but he'd found something in this distance that seemed to promise renewal. Renewal comes in many forms, he knew, and he welcomed its brutality. Carolus always felt closest to God when he could never be forgiven by anyone else. Though he sometimes wondered if even God had a limit to the kind of soul He would redeem. There was something sharp and daunting at the end of it all. Maybe Istanbul would be where he finally saw his future.

When it got dark, Carolus drove in the direction of a walled, vanilla town built into a hill. It was accessed by a series of fluorescent red roads that felt artificial, harboring no bumps.

Dim street lamps lined the settlement, bordering the road and the water. He parked close to the dock and headed inland in hopes of finding a hotel. He was just happy to walk. He petted some of the many stray dogs that hunted him during his trip up the mountainside. They'd built the houses right into the rock. Since it was dark, he could see the tallest structures, windmills blinking on and off and lit from the inside.

The mutts tugged at his pant legs. They were hungry. Some of them dropped off in the steeper inclines. They were ragged things that hadn't seen true company in a while. So, with no prospects of food or shelter and realizing he'd driven straight through midnight, Carolus dropped down to his belly, used two of the smaller dogs as willing pillows, and slept.

He wondered what Glugg, the Window Peeper, would do once he climbed to his window and realized he wasn't there. Part of him wanted to think Glugg would be sad—that he'd mourn the loss of a fellow pervert, outcast, motherfucker—but he'd probably just try to catch a glimpse of Cass a few houses down. Carolus envied him.

CHAPTER 18

December 22
Gáttapefur: Doorway Sniffer

Carolus woke with the taste of hair on his tongue. Raising his hands to his face, he realized rocks had dimpled his cheeks and that his canine pillows had wandered off. He got up and walked back toward the Skylark. On the way, he noticed a food cart that hadn't been there the night before. "Whatcha got?" he asked the old man behind the counter.

"Meat," the vendor answered. He sat on a colorful tin foldout chair with his body facing the water.

"I'll have that. You know the way to Istanbul?"

"Toward Turkey, I'd think," he said, scratching his gray mutton chops.

"That Greek humor?"

"None better," the vendor said, tossing lamb on the grill. He upturned his nose. "You smell like shit."

Carolus rubbed under his armpits. "You're a real fucking darling, you know that?"

"Best way to Istanbul is by boat. By boat you don't need a passport. EU. Helicopters are faster, but you need a passport and sometimes they crash." The vendor scooped up the piece of lamb with a pita and wrapped it in foil. He topped it with a white sauce. "Ella. Four."

"Ella?"

The man just laughed.

Carolus remembered he didn't have any euros on him, so he tossed the keys to the Skylark on the grill and walked away.

* * *

It was too hot for Christmastime. Carolus's thoughts drifted. He imagined the way he and Door Sniffer would sometimes meet—both huddled at the step of his neighbor's bathroom door, breathing deep like hounds and catching the scent of her filth. Women smell different just before they bathe, Carolus thought.

Plagued by chronic back problems, Door Sniffer's abilities had declined in recent years. He'd taught Carolus the fine points of tracking, but his ailment now prevented him from placing his nose wholly beneath the door. So, he'd become more attracted to bolder scents—goats, soured milk, German tourists. Forsaking his red suit for more traditional Icelandic clothes, Door Sniffer was sometimes hard to distinguish from any other arthritic senior. His cane made him easy to hear, so stories spread that children often watched him struggle and teased him.

Two years back, Carolus set a glass of whisky under his door and lured Door Sniffer in for a drink. They sat and talked about the failing economy and Carolus's sexual encounters. Sniffer confessed he hadn't loved a woman in years; instead, he tended to his orchids.

That night, Carolus took Sniffer out to a bar and introduced him to Emir, a woman he knew would perform any number of vile sexual acts. He didn't see Sniffer last Christmas, and he wondered if maybe he'd contracted something and if that should be on his conscience.

CHAPTER 19

"Your Goal is the Fire" — The Koran

When he got to Istanbul, the first thing Carolus smelled was sea bass. The captain told everyone to get off the boat, but there was a lot of shoving and then waiting. Carolus hated waiting ever since it took six weeks for him to receive his Dick Tracy radio watch when he was nine. Like pop music and dance crazes, Dick Tracy had reached Iceland much later than in America.

"What are you going to do with a radio watch, anyway?" his mother had asked.

"I'll listen to people while I'm traveling like Jack Kerouac." For a moment he was impressed with himself that he'd known about the Beats, but then he remembered his mother told him Jack Kerouac wasn't the postman's name.

He remembered talking to Cass about the hairy-eared Asian man who used to run the local drug store when they were kids. She was very upset when he informed her his name wasn't Akira Kurosawa.

"That's a director," he said.

"That's funny that a famous director has the same name as the only Asian person in Reykjavik," she said.

Cass was simple sometimes in a way that made her vulnerable.

When he got off the boat, Carolus headed straight for a cab. He'd settle into his hotel, which he'd booked for the twenty-second. He figured he'd be there a day earlier and call Samsa, who would tell him where to pick up his gun and other materials. From there, he'd head to DHL to receive the package containing the mark's information. Everything was so commercial now. Before, sensitive materials used to be left in safe deposit boxes or under the rails of a train station. Now, everybody was in on it.

When he got in, he told the driver the destination, and the man stepped on the gas and offered him gum. It tasted exotic, like lavender. The city was so huge and still dark, with only a glint of light from the east that made everything glow yellow and pink. The mosques, illuminated in the distance, made him feel the presence of a foreign god.

After a while, he realized the *taksi* driver had run up the meter, and now he was writing strange numbers on his hand, none of which resembled the amount on the meter. "My friend," he repeated, with his hand extended. Carolus handed him 40 YTL, which Samsa had given him before the trip. He was staying at the Old Town Pub Hotel, situated halfway between Sultanahmet and Beyoglu—the ancient and the reborn.

He'd been told this was a good area to disappear in. The elevator up to his room was tiny and metal, and people had keyed things in Turkish. Forbidden words like love, cocksucker, room service.

Stepping outside, Carolus crossed over the Bosphorus to Beyoglu toward Istiklal Caddesi, the biggest road in Istanbul. Along the Galata, hundreds of fishermen caroused over street vendor corn and kebab.

Carolus felt the urge to piss. Many of the fishermen spilled their bait water onto the bridge, and he thought again of Cass. She'd taken him to the lake to fish when they were young and hungry.

He recalled the fountain bed of the green-lilied water and moonfish, which, more often than not, only nibbled on the thick night crawlers dangling from his hook. With a sudden disgust, he'd reel it in and inspect the worm's writhing midsection. It would soon crust and die; Carolus couldn't imagine a more horrifying, unnatural death than that.

Cass had taught him how to cast and how to drink, and because she knew he would learn no other way, how to kiss.

She sat him down on a long flat rock a few inches away from her. She got down on her knees and the wet grass stained her jeans, dark, cool water rising up her thighs. Carolus wondered if an elf lived under the rock. Cass grabbed his jaw tightly and straightened his head because it was drooping with embarrassment.

"You can't tell Mama. She doesn't like these things," Cass said.

Carolus nodded. He remembered his shameful excitement. He shifted his tight white underwear covertly. She leaned in slowly and kissed him on the lips. With her own lips, she adjusted his, and they arrived at a very comfortable standstill. She tasted like red liquorish, and Carolus knew that kiss would become the standard bearer for all kisses to come. He would measure all lips against hers.

Static hissed overhead as if the clouds were deflating. A chant began as part of a nightly prayer. There was something very haunting about listening to someone's confession over a loudspeaker. Carolus felt very alone. He looked out over the water. There must have been fifty ships, most sailing east as if nothing had changed for a thousand years. He lit a cigarette and his stomach burbled because he'd hardly eaten on the boat. He didn't feel anonymous anymore. Carolus wondered if praying truly absolved anyone or if it only led to further prayer. He wondered what Turkish girls liked to do in bed and if it was very different from the rest. He'd seen a picture once on a bondage site of a Turkish girl who'd disobeyed her master, but maybe she was Albanian. He'd heard of women who could change their nationality based on the temperature, like ancient lizards.

Istanbul had become something very large in his mind. And it *was* large. As he walked toward Istiklal, he noticed cats where dogs should have been. They took the place of lights and parking meters. Oblivious to people except for tourists who fed them gum and flowers, the cats ran the city at night. They were loud and gangly. He caught a glimpse of police lights and turned into an alley with several small restaurants and shops. They must have been on to him, he figured. But did they know his face? How much had his shadow given them?

Carolus sat down at a local restaurant with his back against a corner, away from the windows. He checked over his shoulder furtively. The building facade had been recently painted red, but it was a shoddy job, and the metal showed underneath. Carolus ordered lamb brain, meat, and Raki on the waiter's recommendation.

"My friend, you must try the brain. When did you arrive? It doesn't matter; you must try the brain," the waiter said.

So, Carolus tried the brain, and cats leapt at his feet, shimmying in through the open windows. There were at least six of them in the restaurant, which he realized had only one other customer: a balding man wearing a shirt with the name "Mr. Delicious" on it.

The dish tasted utterly like brain, a malty, parsnip-like flavor, but maybe he should've expected that. Though puffin didn't taste like puffin and whale didn't taste like whale. Only chicken was supposed to taste like itself, he thought. His mother used to say, "Never eat anything you wouldn't have slept next to." Maybe she was right.

The waiter returned. "How is everything, my friend?"

Carolus took a big gulp of Raki, and it was strong. It burned the back of his throat. "This brain is fucking terrible."

"Yes, but in Istanbul, you have to try the brain," he said. "I see you've noticed Mr. Delicious. Would you like an introduction?"

"I'm OK."

"He's a celebrity of local import. He makes the finest Turkish Delight on the European side of Istanbul. You must meet him."

The waiter tapped Mr. Delicious on the shoulder and whispered something in his ear. Mr. Delicious sucked in his belly and waddled over. "I have heard you are not Turkish. Is this true?"

Carolus took a bite of meat. "I'm not from a lot of places."

"Is Turkey one of these?"

"Yes." He pushed the brain to one side of his plate next to the brown lemon. Outside, a spattering of rain softened the sidewalks. The cats mewed. Carolus admired the women in the back, white shawls over their heads. They were kneading bread and mixing it with green herbs.

"I am Mr. Delicious."

"What makes you so sure?"

"Yes," he said. "You believe." He turned around and showed Carolus the back of his shirt.

"Well, what makes you so delicious then?"

Mr. Delicious turned to the waiter as if he didn't understand. The waiter spoke to him in Turkish, and he nodded. "In Istanbul it is never appropriate to question the deliciousness of another man."

"I guess that's not really appropriate in Reykjavik either," Carolus conceded.

"So, we are in agreement. You come by my shop tomorrow. You see." He handed Carolus his card, which featured all Turkish words except for the name. "Your name?"

"Boston," Carolus said, "like the city. Anywhere to drink around here?"

But Mr. Delicious had already went back to his table.

The waiter sauntered over with the check. "You follow the music, my friend."

* * *

The waiter didn't know anything about food, but apparently, he knew about booze. Carolus followed the music past meat vendors and stopped at a sign that read "fortune-telling rabbits." Two rabbits stared at each other, and behind them a blind man rambled in a foreign language.

"How much?"

The man held up two fingers, so Carolus gave him all the coins he had. It seemed to be enough. The alleyway was dark, but enough light came off the street that he could see the rabbits. The man fed each bunny a lettuce leaf as they stared at Carolus. The duo waited for a couple of minutes. Carolus thought of leaving, but eventually the rabbit on the right shat out a message. "Alle," the man said, and Carolus picked it up. It smelled OK, he thought, like compost.

It read:

It is unwise to look for meaning in the anus of a rabbit.

"Are you fucking kidding?" Carolus considered grabbing his coins, but the second rabbit excreted another fortune.

A member of your family will soon do something that will make you proud.

It made him happy to think about Cass, so he decided to move toward the music again. He wondered which fortune he should listen to. In a cobblestone alley, tables and chairs with hookah pipes surrounded a mismatched guitar band and several beautiful women—some with large men, some with each other—who clapped along to slinky Arabic music. The blue awning above it read 'Barabar' in all uppercase letters. Carolus sat and ordered Raki.

He ordered one after another. Some of the women noticed him, some didn't. He met a man who'd bicycled from Wales to Istanbul. When his ride finally gave in, he'd crashed into a welder who fixed his wheels for six pieces of English toffee.

From where Carolus sat, he watched little boys pushing barrels of popcorn and raw oysters along the road, and beggars, rarely with all their fingers, sang old sailing songs to cats in exchange for salmon chunks.

He went inside to use the bathroom. Through a long corridor where they kept canned figs and pineapple juice, he found a payphone. It was an old-style payphone like the ones used in 1930s American films like *It Happened One Night*. Carolus was never Clark Gable, though—not even in his fantasies.

He picked up the phone and dialed Samsa. Got the info. Hung up. He kept his hand on the base of the phone and leaned into the booth, where he felt safe. Through the glass, he looked out on the smoke and gyration outside. He called home.

"This could only be one person," a familiar, grating voice said.

"Bjorn, put Cass on."

"You know normal people sleep at night. Normal people have jobs." The cattle dog coughed and whined. "Now you've woken the dog."

"Put Cass on, Bjorn."

"You know—"

A static rustling cut him off.

"Carolus, is that you?" Cass sounded sleepy. Maybe it was later there, but that didn't seem right. He'd forgotten what time it was and it suddenly became morning outside.

"Cass. It's fucking good to hear you."

"You're drunk, Christmas Carolus," she said.

"*You're* drunk," he said. He could hear Bjorn's voice in this background: *No respect for people's lives.*

She shooshed him. She gulped water loudly over the speaker. "Where in all's hell are you? Are you back for the holidays?"

"I'm in Istanbul—at the Old Town Pub Hotel, room 4F. So, don't worry." He liked that someone still worried for him.

"Well, come home."

"Gotta work. They have fortune telling rabbits and corn here. You should come."

"Don't be stupid. How can corn tell the future? Are you eating OK?" she asked.

And just at that moment, Carolus saw the girl he'd created back in the Dutch pub with the driver and the passenger. He swore she looked the same, and here she was: outside, alone, dancing with her hands up in the air to the morning music. He dropped the phone onto the receiver. He must have been hallucinating, he thought.

When Carolus first saw her, he trembled, a great pain in his stomach—partially from the meat sandwich in oil he'd eaten earlier, the Raki, and from something he could only describe as the terrible gassiness of desire.

Her hair was sweet corn blonde, and the small spots that appeared on her face in the light did not detract from her beauty. She was slender, dressed modestly in jeans and a silk canary blouse that didn't reveal her cleavage. Her skin was pale but distinctly foreign. Her dimples made her seem wholesome, but he should have known she wasn't since he'd created her.

Her eyes had not seen Europe.

He went up and kissed her and she slapped him. He kissed her again and she held his hand.

"What's your name?" she asked. He could hardly believe that such things were possible. He'd always wondered about the creation of things. He wondered why God chose to rest on the seventh day. He felt tremendous power that she owed him her life and her soul. "Carolus," he offered and pointed to his chest.

She nodded. "Aschel," she said. Her accent was pretty and thick. She started speaking Turkish, sounding similar to Mr. Delicious. He wondered if he was betraying Delia. Then he realized how stupid he was. Delia didn't belong to him. A great many things could change in the coming days, but he didn't even know where Delia was or if she was alive, thanks to his carelessness.

Carolus called over the waiter, a tall man who'd razored his beard into tiny zebra-like lines. "What's she saying?"

The waiter listened. "She says she thinks you are a silly man."

"I am. Tell her."

The waiter told her, but his attention waned from the conversation as a group of young women sat in his section. "She says, 'Why do you look at me like you have already penetrated me?'"

"She said that?" Carolus frowned. He hadn't imagined such unclean words could come out of the mouth he'd given her. "Tell her I think she's—I dreamt her up."

"She says many men have dreamt her over the years."

Carolus lit a cigarette. "Are you sure you told her *dreamt*?"

"Yes, 'dreamt,' sir. She says what do you want to do with her? Excuse me." The waiter went off to the table of women.

"To do with you?" He placed his hand around her waist. He thought again of Delia and how maybe he should be searching for her. But where would he even begin? He had a job to accomplish and he could start his search afterward. His train of thought was broken when he glimpsed two Turkish policemen about a hundred meters away. They wore baby blue short-sleeved shirts and black pants. One carried a submachine gun while the other probably only had his holstered pistol. They hadn't noticed him yet.

"We have to go!" he barked, rising up.

Aschel didn't seem to understand. He made a motion like wings with his hands and pointed furtively at the police. He grabbed her wrist, and she didn't resist. Maybe she liked danger, he thought. If so, she was in luck.

Back in his hotel room, he threw her over a chair and took her from behind. It was funny, Carolus thought, to hear screams in a different language—of pleasure, or maybe he was a little rough. But she seemed to like it.

She played dirty games of hide the pickle and the police chief and the seamstress. Games he'd invented as a teenager. Everything about Aschel, especially her thighs, seemed fresh.

Afterward, she drew him a picture of a sailboat and seemed pleased. She spoke for a little while, but very little resembled English. Frustrated, she dialed down to the front desk. Ten minutes later, a bellhop arrived. She spoke a few sentences to him. Carolus thought it was immodest because they were still naked in bed and the kid was just standing there a little in shock—maybe because Aschel wasn't covered up well and the sight of her was like looking into the sun.

Carolus pulled the sheet over her thighs so the boy could concentrate. He liked how her hips moved when she talked.

"The lady says that you are a master of sexual things and you have a . . ." he hesitated, "a member like that of a much larger mammal." He seemed uncomfortable translating.

Carolus smiled. He enjoyed her grapefruit scent. "Tell her she's god-damn spectacular, but I gotta meet someone for business."

He told her. Her legs tightened under the covers.

"You can go now," Carolus said.

The boy left. Carolus got out of bed, put on some socks and boxers, a white button down, a clean pair of slacks, and an overcoat. He stretched his hands in the air and she pouted.

"I'll be back for you."

Before he left, she lifted the sheets and flashed her tiny bush. He adjusted himself in the lobby and ordered her blueberry crepes.

CHAPTER 20

Each section of Istanbul had become specialized over the centuries. The metal section where every part of every machine sat in plastic bins, the socket store, the light bulb factory, the plastic doll head mart, the leather emporiums, candy road, and, finally, the Pet Bazaar where Samsa's contact sold sickly gerbils.

It was a good place to get lost. The bazaar housed countless beasts humping away in cages. Hair, straw, and birdseed mottled the ground. The matted huff of wet fur softened the hooting. A straw thatching hung overhead so that only some of the cool winter sun bent through. Set up like a hedge maze, the space smelled of feces and trail mix.

A few peddlers in Chico Marx hats offered Carolus chickens. "Are you Spanish?" they asked. "No? We love the Spanish, my friend. You love the chicken?"

"Which one?" he asked quietly and walked away.

The gerbil stand rested between horse mackerel and baby rattlers. Carolus stepped toward the vendor. "You Samsa's boy?"

He wasn't really paying enough attention to give an answer. He was thinking of Aschel's ass and how perfectly jelly donut-round it was. Round in a good way. Round in the da Vinci sense.

Almost anything seemed appealing on her skin. And yet, it was hard to shake the feeling that he'd already fallen for someone and she'd been taken from him. Aschel seemed more and more his own creation. A woman of desperation.

When the boy was through jabbering, he motioned to Carolus to follow. He followed the vendor's dirty head through the crowd. The vendor wore a yellow bandana, which made it easier, but suddenly, the crowd parted and Carolus stepped aside. A small coffin, the size of a dog or maybe a chimpanzee, carried by three strong men, barreled down the center of the bazaar. Everyone seemed to know who or what rested inside. Some prayed, but most simply stared at the box as you would a letter you didn't want to open. It was undeniable that whatever lay in that coffin had profoundly impacted the lives of many Istanbullus. Carolus prayed for its soul.

He mourned the turtles and Gila monsters, too, marked with white crosses on their backs. "What is it?" he asked the vendor.

"They're sick. If they don't sell today, they go in the toilet," he said, picking up speed now that the procession had passed.

Carolus bought a tiny red-eared slider and made the vendor wait for him. He felt slightly redeemed by this act. He slid the turtle in his coat pocket with some food and tiny eye drops that cost 10 YTL extra.

"He has the cataracts. Not out of the water too long," the turtle haggler said.

Carolus nodded and continued with the vendor, who led him through the Grand Bazaar. With doomed ceilings of stained glass lamps the shape of lollipops and the color of prayer, the Bazaar seemed an endless maze of semi-circular enclaves where magic lamps and bronze coffee pots hung, lit golden and shrouded in cigarette smoke. Only white pillars separated one shop from another in the disorder.

"Samsa says you are world class," the vendor said. He took out a small wooden pipe and stuffed it with tobacco as they walked.

"You guys celebrate Christmas here?" They passed a stall of belly dancing outfits: gaudy, sequined bust-huggers, some with longer skirts than others. He wondered what type of women filled out these costumes. The old woman in the stall motioned toward him. Maybe she'd danced ages ago. Carolus knew one day Delia and Aschel's youth would fade like that too. He couldn't bear to think of it. If he never saw Delia again she would always be twenty-nine and sickeningly beautiful, and it would haunt him.

"Christmas is the one with the Easter Bunny, yes?" the vendor asked.

"You're kidding, right?"

"Yes, I kid," he said and stopped at a small Turkish coffee shop on a corner stall shrouded in beads. "We're here." Carolus sat down and the boy poured him a sweet, hot cup. He left for a little, dipped inside the beads and emerged with a small briefcase. "Your materials are inside. I took your liberties of picking up the information because the place is hard to find. You can find it in here, too."

Carolus cracked open the case very slightly so no one else could see its contents. Papers, a Ruger Mark II with a silencer, a wig, fake passport, fresh clothes, and ten thousand euros and lira. He shut it. "What do I owe you?"

"Samsa took care of that. Pay him upon return. I told him, 'What if he meets the maker of things?' and he said, 'Carolus cannot die because he's not done suffering. He hasn't even begun it.' This is what he said in his words."

"Well, at least he's got faith in me," Carolus said, downing the scalding coffee. He picked up the briefcase and left as the vendor vanished behind the beads.

CHAPTER 21

Carolus decided to change and check on Aschel before he contacted the mark. He was hungry by the time he got back to Beyoglu. Several cats followed him as he walked and sweated up the staircase alleys of Istanbul. By the time he got back to the hotel, he was ready for sex and dinner. Then, he'd have to go finish his work. He wasn't used to being hunted. He couldn't go home now if he wanted to.

Carolus entered the hotel, but, to his stunned surprise, the girl who came to the door at the turn of his key was Cass.

"Jesus God. What are you doing here?" Carolus panicked. All of his worlds crashed together. He was both happy to see her and terrified of the danger she knew nothing of. Behind her in the hotel room, he only saw plates of uneaten crepes soaked in butter and marzipan. The space was small, with the bathroom to the right of the entrance. The eggshell-colored room opened out into a twin bed on the left and a mirror with lilies in front of it across the way. An Oriental rug that seemed completely out of place sat between the bed and the TV stand. A window looked out onto the street, but someone had drawn the shades.

Aschel was gone. A flutter of gnats swarmed up behind Cass, and Carolus's mind flashed to that blood-covered poseable Jesus. He pulled back and hugged her in the doorway, sniffed her perfume, which had been the same since she was fourteen. There was comfort in holding her and he thought of his mother saying *not too long, now*. Maybe she blamed him for a lot more than he remembered. As he entered the room, he breathed heavily and went straight to the bathroom.

He dropped his briefcase on the bathroom tile, opened the envelope.

It was Mr. Delicious. The mark was Mr. Fucking Delicious. Carolus felt relieved. He even laughed a little for such a ridiculous character. Who could be angry with Mr. Delicious? he wondered. It could've been Astrid, the old man with the rabbits, or some poor rocking horse vendor who looked at the guy the wrong way on Christmas. But it was Mr. Delicious, and Carolus was content. He came out of the bathroom and put his forehead against Cass's and asked her how she was.

"I'm missing Christmas for you, asshole," she said.

He hugged her again. "You didn't see a blonde girl here, did you?"

"That's who let me in. I tried to say who I was, but she just ran off." Cass wore a silver necklace he'd given her a few birthdays back that he liked on her. It hugged her neckline.

"What are you doing here?" he asked. "It's nice to see you."

"You told me to come. You gave me your hotel number. We just jumped on a plane. So impulsive. Bjorn never does things like this!"

"Oh right, of course," he lied, not recalling the conversation with any clarity.

Cass could always tell when he was fibbing. "You were drunk. It's a very dirty city, isn't it? Did you see the baby doll head store?"

"I saw it, yes." He reached into his coat pocket and offered her the turtle. Its tiny feet churned against his cradling hand.

"Why's it marked white?"

"He's not well. Where's Bjorn?" Carolus sat on the bed and rested the creature on his thigh. He dripped eye drops into its tiny, milky pupils.

Cass leaned against the white bathroom door. "You know what Mama would say. Your pets always ended up dead." She stared past him in a way she had many years before. It was the same way their mother would stare past him when she was mad. An aggressively distant gaze.

"Yeah, well, who would've thought that goddamn cattle dog would outlive her?" Carolus snapped. He regretted it almost immediately, as if he'd tarnished something beautiful. "What is it that you think I do, Cass?" He felt the raw truth bubbling from his chest. There had been a myriad of moments when he'd wanted to tell her about his work. It was hard to hide from her, and yet he'd done it all these years. He wanted her to be proud.

"You want me to know what you do? You never seemed to before. Just importing and exporting, you said."

He stretched his arms as far apart as they could go and curled his toes. He thought of Mr. Delicious. Poor, good-as-dead Mr. Delicious and how it might be funny if the situation were a game show. He envisioned a live studio audience reacting as he landed the fatal blow.

"I met a girl, Cass."

"You always meet a girl."

He realized that he meant Delia and not Aschel. "It's strange that you're here by yourself. What about the uncles?" Carolus thought of Christmas now embodied in her. He wondered if she could smell the latex and sweat in the room and felt ashamed.

Cass curled her body next to Carolus, her head by his knees, tinkering with the red-eared slider. "What are you going to do with him?"

"I was thinking of keeping him."

The closer she moved her finger, the more the turtle retracted his head until it vanished. "I'm not alone, of course. Bjorn's checking our bags and buying spring water."

Carolus brushed his sister's white hair out of her eyes. She'd cut it a little and he didn't like that. There was a dullness in her expression that felt sad and distant, and he knew something had happened to her to make her come. "Something happen back home?"

She hesitated as if contemplating whether or not to lie. "Do you ever wonder what it would be like if we weren't brother and sister?" She snapped up the turtle and set off into the bathroom without closing the door. Cass ran lukewarm water and placed it in the sink. She rubbed her eyes in the mirror.

"Like how?"

"You ever think about how there might be completely different versions of us out there, like one of those funhouse mirrors or the little Morton's salt girl?"

"What are you doing?"

"Getting ready to go out. It's not always that your sister's in Istanbul with you," she said, shutting the bathroom door. She turned on the hotel hairdryer, probably just to sit with it. It was something she did as a girl when she wanted privacy.

He got up and leaned against the door, listening. "You're not staying here are you?" he yelled. She must not have been able to hear him.

Someone knocked at the door. Carolus sighed, annoyed to have to see Bjorn. When he opened up, a stranger about five inches his better jabbed him in the chest and threw him backward. As his neck smacked the bed frame, the man lunged at him. He choked Carolus, who struggled to work his hands under the man's arms.

Losing consciousness and out of breath, Carolus spit in the attacker's eye and kneed him repeatedly in the groin until the man's grip loosened. The fight stopped as they both caught their breath. The attacker lay on top of Carolus, the two of them limply staring at each other like paralyzed bears. Carolus flipped the attacker over. It took four good flat-handed shots to shatter his nose. A spurt of blood splattered Carolus's gray button-down.

The attacker still fought back, but his spirit seemed broken. Maybe he was especially proud of his nose.

"You motherfucker. Gregory was a good man," he panted.

"Gregory. What about Tomas?"

The assailant looked confused. Carolus took the opportunity to swing his elbow violently into the man's forehead and knock him unconscious, leaving him bleeding on the floor.

Carolus knocked on the bathroom door to check on Cass. She shut off the hair dryer. "I'm almost ready. What are you doing out there anyway?"

"You keep getting ready; just hand me my briefcase?"

"Don't look, OK?" She cracked open the door and fit the briefcase through the slit.

Carolus was a little offended that she had to ask. He opened the case, took a peek at Mr. Delicious's picture, screwed the silencer on the gun, and shot his attacker twice in the head. He wrapped him with the orange bedspread along with the rug and shoved the body and his own stained shirt under the bed. His hands were bloody, so he slid them into his pockets. Gregory. Carolus thought about it for a moment. The driver? Who would try to kill him next? he wondered.

Cass exited wearing an off-white cocktail dress that cut off just before her knees. She matched the room. Cass frowned. "What's going on in here? You're sweating. This room looks all messy all of a sudden. Were you . . ." Cass inspected the room.

"Was I what?" Carolus felt goddamn stupid for answering the door so nonchalantly. He wasn't just looking out for himself anymore. He stood in front of the bloodspots, covering the silenced Ruger with the bedspread.

"Were you masturbating?" Cass whispered, although there was no one else in the room. No one she knew about, anyway.

Carolus smiled, in a scattered, relieved way. "Thought I could squeeze one in. Literally."

"Gross." She frowned.

"You've got a smudge," Carolus said, pointing to her eyeliner.

"Where's your shirt?"

"What? You don't like?" He patted his belly before quickly retracting his hands.

She laughed a little. "God forgive you," she said. "You're intolerable."

Cass went back into the bathroom.

Guy must've had a cold, he thought, rubbing his slimy fingers against his palms. "We've gotta run." Carolus locked his case and changed his shirt. He asked Cass to pluck the turtle from the sink in the bathroom and place it in his coat pocket. The paint had dissolved in the water, turning it a milky white.

When they got downstairs, Carolus slipped the bellhop 100 YTL. "I won't be needing my room cleaned, understand?" Carolus wiped blood from his mouth.

The boy nodded anxiously.

He caught up to Cass outside.

"What happened to your lip?" she asked.

"I bit it when I heard Bjorn was coming," Carolus said.

"You are *so* very funny."

Outside, Carolus nudged Cass into a cab and told the cabbie to drive for a while, knowing he'd probably been waiting to hear that all his life—an open fare.

"What about Bjorn?" Cass asked.

"We'll leave word at the hotel when we get where we're going. You two have your own room, yes?"

"Yes. This city smells like meat," she said.

"We are high in meat saturation here," the cab driver said.

"Don't listen to the cabbies here," Carolus whispered. He was relieved that Bjorn wouldn't walk in on the dead assailant and the one hundred insured no one else would. "You look nice," he said after a pause.

She punched him playfully in the shoulder and it really hurt his neck. He was sore all over from the skirmish. It started to snow.

"I bring the weather with me," Cass said. "It's colder than usual back home. Uncle Asgeir is upset we're gone."

"Does he still have that gland problem?"

"I don't think that's something you get over."

"That's too bad," Carolus said. He thought of Mr. Delicious's head. It was a large one, perhaps inflated from sugars and alcohol. He'd deal with him soon.

"You should go to Galata Tower," the driver said. "It is for non-locals such as yourselves and they will put on shows and food. Dancers."

He remembered the outfits at the bazaar. Carolus nodded, disregarding his own advice. The driver took a left.

When they got to the tower, he tossed the *taksi* driver fifty lira and that seemed to be enough. He didn't want to haggle.

* * *

Cass climbed the tower's stone-winding stairs in silence. When they reached the top, the maître d' seated them near the stage where they sat surrounded by Ukrainians. The maître d' was a man in his mid-forties and had a small hunch, making his black jacket ride up in the back. Each table reflected the nation of its attendees, so it was nice to see the miniature Icelandic flag next to their red wine and pita. The stage resembled a small crescent: surrounded like stars by about fifty white-clothed tables.

They drank for a while and ate nameless meats as several knife throwers performed on stage in puffy attire. The audience gasped with every throw.

"What happened with Bjorn?" Carolus asked, tearing a piece of pita bread and stuffing it in his mouth.

"Bjorn and I aren't in love anymore, I think," she said, hiding her lips behind her glass. Her white hair framed her pale face. She wore little dangly earrings, a pair Carolus gave her when he was fifteen.

The statement was blunt and unexpected. Usually, Cass was so measured. "I'm sorry to hear that," he said, not intending to mean it. He did mean it a little, though. She seemed unhappy.

"Why'd you bring him then?" He snatched the turtle from his coat and dropped it into a glass of water. It sank to the bottom of the glass, then pushed itself up to the surface with its back flippers.

"Last ditch—that sort of thing. It was either this or have a baby."

Carolus downed a glass of wine and motioned to the waiter for another. His attention shifted as belly dancers took the stage. There were three of them, dark beauties. They moved fluidly, and he thought back to nights of prayer and masturbation in the small caves by the park. They were tough to reach, and he'd bring cheese, cherry juice, and his mother's lingerie catalogues. It was so cold that sometimes he couldn't climax, but it was beautiful to watch the icefall. Once, a rabbit took shelter with him. They hid from the moon together.

In Iceland, the twenty-third of December is St. Thorlakur's Day. Carolus remembered meeting hairless men who stood on tall rocks on the outskirts of town and called themselves prophets. They preached to large, intoxicated crowds by bonfire light and bottle rockets.

Carolus felt uninspired by the belly dancing and awkward because Cass wanted him to say something that would mend her, but he knew he couldn't. Then the lead dancer entered. She glided toward him, midriff glittering, her satin pants revealing vertical slits from waist to ankle. She was chained to the sultan's arm as if in a harem and she was wickedly gorgeous—familiar, even. Cutting through the shadows and her deep rouge, Carolus realized the dancer was Delia.

He felt both guilt and excitement. He wondered if it could be a coincidence. He downed another glass of wine and sucked tabouli off his thumb.

"You know that girl, too?" Cass said, incredulously.

"What do you mean 'too'?"

"Jesus. I hope you, you know, protect the merchandise." Cass, who wasn't much of a drinker, gulped too much wine.

"It's almost Christmas," Carolus said as if just realizing its significance.

As if by fate, the sultan asked for volunteers to dance in the harem. Carolus leapt out of his seat. He bounded onto the stage, excited to see Delia up close again, to smell her again; when she perspired, it smelled like Apple Jacks.

He introduced himself as Boston to the crowd. As he did, Delia's thighs and knuckles tightened.

In a line with the other dancers, he mimicked their movements to the amusement of the crowd and whispered to Delia. "I didn't think I'd see you again."

"This is a city of mystics, don't you know that?"

"Do you know who's trying to kill me?" Carolus swung his hips and the crowd cheered for him. He felt out of breath.

"Who'd want to kill you?" she asked, eyeing the sultan.

"That's funny."

The sultan pulled at Delia's chains. She faced forward.

"Who's he?"

"I've thought about you. Did you come here to save me?" she asked.

"I'm rarely on that end of things," Carolus said, slightly puzzled at her request.

"Who is the lady you're with?"

The sultan tugged on her chain again and she yelped.

Carolus shoved the sultan. "Don't fuck with the girl."

The other dancers stopped. The sultan shoved him back and the crowd let out a collective gasp. Carolus punched the sultan in the head, took Delia by the chain, and grabbed Cass and the glass with the turtle. The maître d' and a waiter chased after them down the long, winding staircase while he shouted profanities at them. "Mouse dicks! Weevils!"

By the time they got to the bottom of the tower, they were out of breath and Delia shivered in her skimpy dancing attire. Carolus threw his blazer around her shoulders. She kissed him on the cheek.

"The hell is going on?" Cass demanded. "Are you insane? Why did you ruin the show?"

"Hi, I'm Delia." She took Cass's hand.

Carolus figured it was better to run than fight, so he told Cass to take off her heels and follow; Delia was already shoeless. They ran downhill, and, in the distance, across the Galata Bridge where Asia met Europe in the golden minareted skyline, the lights began to fail. Slowly, darkness crept up on the group until it enclosed them. They scampered down alleyways with nothing in front of them but the candlelight of faraway mosques.

Cass said she stepped on something slimy, so they stopped. Carolus said he needed to think. Delia, in the darkness, placed his hands on her warm hips, barely covered, sweaty. He ran his hand down her thigh. There was something satisfying about touching her right in front of Cass. He slipped his fingers inside her and she curved back onto him, her thick hair catching on his scruff.

CHAPTER 22

December 24
Kertasnikir: Candle Beggar

Back in the days when candles were made of animal fat, the Candle Beggar was a plump, inquisitive Lad entranced by the glow and taste of candles that bent the limbs of evergreens all over Iceland. Now emaciated and nearing his end of days, Carolus would sometimes see the Candle Beggar sucking on old menorahs, long since devoid of sustenance. He lived like a vagabond, staring longingly into brightly lit Christmas displays and pining for a forgotten time. He wore a long lambskin coat, all white, which made his beard even more fantastic like the red poppy oil Cass would sometimes rub under her breasts and armpits before a date.

Sometimes, Carolus would trim the turkey fat off his meal and stick a candlewick on top. This would keep the Candle Beggar's search alive—keep him believing that perhaps his time on this earth hadn't passed.

* * *

Carolus managed to find a cheap hotel for Cass and Delia and said for them to ring Bjorn and become friends before he came back for Christmas Eve dinner. He sent for Cass's bags, too.

As morning passed over the Bosphorus, Carolus imagined Delia's voice as one of prayer sounding over the grainy speakers and echoing through the writhing city. It was hard for him to imagine lusting after anyone else, even Aschel, but he tried so he wouldn't forget. A great terror overtook him as he imagined forgetting the small pieces of humanity that he'd clung to over the years. The backs of his hands had grown hairy like a wolf's. There was a small part of him that believed no truly human person could live with the things he'd done.

He wondered what he'd do with Cass and if they'd talk about him while he was gone. Of course they'd talk. Women talk.

He felt like maybe each time he fucked a girl, he was trying to catch her up on everything she'd missed. Each time he said the word love and she discovered the moles and imperfections on his body, each time he told another woman about his mother and accepted her meek condolences, those memories made up a lifetime. If he could put every love affair he'd ever had together like some skin-coated jigsaw puzzle, it would all add up to Carolus.

He was happy to have Delia again. He tried to remember being inside of her, but he only tasted Raki and heard the slap of his waist against her thighs in the darkness. He felt hollowed out by this discovery.

As he walked toward Old Town where Mr. Delicious set up shop, he remembered talking to his father.

"When you're old, you'll see how stupid it is what you wish for your whole life," his father said, drinking cocoa in his favorite brown chair. A cigarette burned slowly in an ashtray next to him. He had the fatigued look that all fathers get on Sunday afternoons.

Carolus didn't recall having any cocoa. "What do I wish for?"

"A warm place to hide," he said, staring out the front window into the bare yard.

"Such as a camel?" Carolus asked.

"You and me, kid, we're on the same wavelength. Let me tell you."

"Camels are good. So are Cass and erasers."

"Erasers are pretty good, yeah," his father mumbled, leaning back, tucking his shirt down into his trousers.

Carolus tried to remember his father's cologne or the color of his fingernails, but each proved elusive in its own way. They each blended with the oily scent of a black and white matinee the pair had seen on a snowy Tuesday and the long-corroded dreams Carolus suffered after his death.

* * *

A cool breeze picked up. It carried the ocean with it. Carolus walked into Old Town. Each building in the area resembled a child's coloring book: patterns of pastels and polka dots worn from the ice and the summer heat. Old women, their heads wrapped in silken scarves, poked their dark, tired faces out into the wind, hanging long dresses that had been passed down for generations on clothes lines between houses. Bars adorned the windows, and the streets seemed to flow downward like playground slides emptying at the Bosphorus.

Walking south, Carolus reached the confectionary shop. Above the shop, a sign read *Mr. Delicious* and said something in Turkish under-neath. It was clear he was in the right spot. From across the street, he watched two similar-looking men shovel candy into paper bags for a steady stream of customers. They stored each delight in identical glass jars that they covered with bronze, nipple-like lids. The shop wasn't ideal, Carolus thought. Too many witnesses, a cashier: too messy. Green and red candies dominated the selections, but he spotted rose, mastic, pista-chio, too—all muted by a thin layer of sifted sugar.

Carolus walked in and a little bell tinkled above the door. He waited behind two customers. Mr. Delicious recognized him. "My friend," he said, "you have understood my deliciousness."

"I guess I have," Carolus said, trying not to look him in the eyes. He had to admit, Mr. Delicious was charming, maybe even likeable. Something about him made you want to eat something sweet and search for fireflies.

"Have you seen Topkapi Palace?" Mr. Delicious asked.

"Not yet."

"Try this." He handed Carolus a pink candy and Carolus placed it in his mouth. At first, because of the sugar, it was dry, but then confection-ary rose hit his tongue. There are few things more nostalgic than the taste of unearned sweets. Carolus let a couple of customers through as Mr. Delicious came out from behind the counter. "This is good, yes?"

"What's in this palace?"

"It is containing the actual footprint of Mohammed, the rod Moses used to fight the desert. The old harem."

"I like harems."

Mr. Delicious fed Carolus another candy. "You seem like a man who is in need of guidance."

Carolus tasted the pasty mint.

"I will tour you around Topkapi."

"I'd like that." It was funny to Carolus that this man's altruistic act would directly lead to his death. Maybe funny wasn't the word, he thought. He felt some remorse for the man's kindness. The Lads had always told him it was good if he didn't enjoy what he was doing. It would be worrisome when he began to crave it. He now teetered on the edge of things. "Tomorrow?"

"Is this not Christmas for you?"

"Not here it's not," Carolus said.

CHAPTER 23

On the way back to the hotel where Cass and Delia waited, Carolus felt the urge to flee. A steady snowfall rained down. He decided to take Istiklal Caddesi, the street he knew best. He didn't really know roads any more except the paths of his youth that had disintegrated in everything but name. He felt impaled by the snow, which was no different in Istanbul than anywhere else that Christmas Eve. If it covered enough, he thought, he could be home again with a view of the frozen sea, only with cats and trolleys slinking down the busy street. Even in the cold, the ice cream men spun their taffy concoctions, enticing young tourists to try an expensive scoop. He could smell the stiff bite of coffee steaming off the sidewalks.

Several cats judged him as he passed. Their eyes grew more yellow with the night. It felt wrong, the snow covering ledges and the tops of small trees along Istiklal. It was supposed to be the edge of Western civilization, he thought. He veered off onto a side street where a group of senior citizens, maybe from Denmark, had gathered to sip apple tea and watch whirling dervishes cloaked in white, spinning perfectly like eggs in the steady drift of snow. Three dervishes spun next to one another. They took breaks every four minutes as a tour guide explained in English that "Dervishes were initiates of the Sufi path, and their dance represented a mystical journey of spiritual ascent through mind and love to what they call 'Perfect.'"

Carolus felt unworthy to have seen perfection. He admired their balance and their ability not to smile. He wondered if they were sterile. They seemed like the kind of men who'd given up their hedonism for a greater ecstasy; Carolus knew no other kind.

A series of linked alleyways somehow circled back to Istiklal. In a few minutes, he was back at the Welcome Feronya Hotel, which didn't make all that much sense to him as a name. It was cheap and secluded. He'd already left one hotel with a body in it—something he knew he'd have to clean up. He was determined not to repeat the sloppy offense.

Inside, Cass and Delia had made a small spread of store-bought food on the bed. They kneeled by empty plates. Bjorn sat in the corner like a child who'd been punished. It was strange to see him without the cattle dog. Carolus walked in and knelt next to them as Cass prayed.

"To never getting old or tired, to never realizing where we are, to never forgetting what brought us here and to Mama and Dad and anyone Delia, too, might be missing. Amen."

Carolus said "amen" and picked at the small plastic bowls of food. She'd left out Bjorn in saying grace. Some deep rift had formed between them.

Carolus felt a little embarrassed. Neither Cass nor his mother had ever been fond of the girls he brought home.

He once traveled to Cologne to see a girl who'd refused to sleep with him after he bought her a necklace. She said it was too sad. When he saw her, they kissed on the cheek and she showed him the Rhine and how sausage was made. They slept with their backs to each other. He remembered how warm she was; the heat coming off her thighs kept him awake all night, incensed with lust.

Now, Carolus looked over the small meal Delia and his sister had prepared. He let himself imagine Delia back in Iceland cooking stew as he poisoned someone. "It's real nice," Carolus said. "You guys did a real nice job." They were both strong, both too good for the men they were with.

"Where were you?" Cass asked.

The L-shaped room was thick and paisley-walled with two beds separated by a nightstand, a bathroom, and a closet in the corner. A square TV and cable box poked out of a pine dresser. The windows looked out to another building. It was eerily similar to the last room but smaller and with one fewer corpse.

"It's interesting how you're always disappearing, brother," Bjorn said.

"You're looking well. Did you do something different with the shape of your head?" Carolus asked.

Bjorn turned toward the window, shunning the food. But as Carolus was about to dip into the creamy ezme, he froze, reflecting on what Bjorn had just called him: "brother," the same way his shadow had addressed him. And why had he come all the way to Istanbul? Carolus began to feel detached from the reality in front of him. He realized that he knew nothing and no one knew him. Could he really suspect his own brother-in-law?

"So, have you gotten everything you wanted, Carolus?" Bjorn asked.

"What is it you think I wanted?" Carolus sat on the windowsill next to Bjorn. He had to decide what to do with him now. Could he kill his brother-in-law? Had the Lads ever said anything about extended family?

"You wanted your sister here. You couldn't bear to be away from her. God forbid she spends a normal Christmas with her husband."

"Is that why you're here? Because of me?"

"It's always been about you, Carolus."

Was that a confession? Carolus's world felt suddenly constricting. He choked on the truth of it all. "How's the soap business?" Carolus asked. It was all coming together. The soap business was about as real as importing and exporting. But how could he do it? How could he square it with Cass? He knew nothing could be done in front of her. Had the entire marriage been a sham?

"Soap will always be necessary." Bjorn seemed distracted, staring out into the wet streets below.

"Have you walked across the Bosphorus yet?"

"We came straight from the airport. I don't sleep on planes." Cavernous rings had formed under his eyes.

"That's a shame. This city's full of mysteries." Carolus glanced protectively at Delia and Cass. The way they were drinking wine, they'd be out in an hour or so. "Why don't you sneak out of here when Cass goes to bed and take a tour with me?" he whispered.

"My goal was all about spending as little time with you as possible."

Cass and Delia laughed to themselves and paid little attention to the men. Carolus realized he could raise his voice to a normal level. "My sister will be thrilled that we did something together when you tell her tomorrow. For now, don't mention it. It'll go a long way toward fixing things. Trust me."

"What do you know about fixing?"

"I've broken enough," Carolus said. He joined the two women and grabbed a glass of wine from Delia, reaching over her back and grazing her breast. He sat behind her and she relaxed, leaning into his chest. A moment later, Bjorn joined them. He nodded to Carolus.

* * *

When the women had sunk into drunken slumber, Bjorn met Carolus outside the motel and they began walking. A cold rain fell steadily, which forced thumb-sized holes in the drift from earlier.

"You and my sister—you're not well I hear," Carolus said. He imagined Bjorn's bloated body. He imagined having Cass all to himself again.

"I miss the dog. I was sorry I couldn't take him. They don't feed him right at the kennel."

"You and that dog have something special." The dog entered Carolus's mind. He couldn't shake its gaze.

As they approached the water, the fishing wharfs creaked hollow against the icy wash. Fishhook lamps on the bridge illuminated small yellowish cones every ten meters. Walking into the light, Carolus lit two cigarettes, held one out for Bjorn.

"I've been cutting back," Bjorn said.

"Now's not a good time."

Bjorn took the cigarette and placed it in his mouth.

"Each relationship is harder than the last, you know? Because you have too much to compare it to," Carolus said.

The hour hit midnight, and a steady, monotone string of prayer hissed over the PA system near the bridge, the voice tucked away somewhere in the recesses of the Blue Mosque. Mr. Delicious's head would roll tomorrow, and Bjorn knew—he must have. It would be a perfect time to set a trap or alert the police. Carolus would have to move before his brother-in-law had a chance to.

As they walked, they passed in and out of the streetlights like specters over the waves. The cigarette cherries flickering in the darkness marked their existence.

"I had this vision the other night of my mother on her deathbed by the sea. These infant whales were beaching themselves onto the shore— writhing and spewing blubber from their gashes onto the black rock. It was such a spectacle I couldn't even listen to what she was saying. The words were falling out of her, and every time I tried to cover her body, she'd throw the sheet right back at me as if she was, I don't know, clinging to that last grim moment. All I wanted was to bury it."

Bjorn looked at Carolus with pity for the first time.

Carolus had revealed the weakness in his soul that he reserved only for the dead.

"Is that how it happened?" Bjorn asked.

"No. Or maybe it is. The sentiment is real, anyway. That makes it true."

"It's a distortion," Bjorn said.

"Do you wish to confess, brother?" Carolus asked.

Bjorn took a long drag and tossed the cigarette over the wooden thigh-high railing to his right. "What did you have in mind?"

"Anything you might want to say before the ears of God?"

The Turkish chanting enveloped them, reverberated in their chests.

"I don't know what I was thinking following you out here. You're just a little weirdo, aren't you? You're just broken."

They passed out of the light. Carolus grabbed Bjorn by the shoulder and held him up against the railing. He hardly struggled as Carolus lifted him and tossed him over the side as if he knew it was coming all along. A faint yelp and then a splash nearly inaudible against the prayer. His body crumpled against the surf. Only Carolus emerged into the blonde lamplight. He leaned over the railing, cigarette sagging in the sleet. He watched the water—how black it was, how contorted—as ribbons of blood foamed like coffee.

CHAPTER 24

December 25
Gryla and the Black Cat

On Christmas Day 1976, Carolus forgot to buy his father a new shirt. It was clear by legend what the consequences would be: death by cat. Cass and his mother glared at him. He was only eight. He now wondered why his mother had given him such severe responsibility. He was just supposed to pick it up from Mrs. Pickswill, the local knitter. She'd woven him a fine sweater from the remains of other garments that had been tossed at the mountain as offerings to the witch, Gryla, and her black mountain cat. It was supposed to be blue, Carolus remembered. He imagined it as a very royal blue that would equal his father's eyes.

Upon unwrapping the last present, a letter opener and not a shirt, his father stared out at the sugar snow that covered everything, even the wolves. He slogged over to the window. "You all are too much," he said.

"Don't you have something for your father?" his mother asked.

Carolus stared at his father's back, framed black by the ice sifting through the curtains. His father opened the window wider so the cold could come in.

His mother grabbed Carolus's shoulder. "You have something for your father!"

But Carolus knew he'd doomed his own father to be eaten by the cat. The black-matted, stinking Yule Cat. He'd always thought it was a myth. What creature would eat the poor who couldn't afford new clothes? But seeing his father make his silent peace, he knew she was real.

From the mountain, Gryla could hear the prayers of men. She designed terrible contraptions to torture the Yule Cat, make her undesirable to other cats, fatten her. The Yule Cat desired blood. Carolus related to this now. He had become a violent instrument.

On Christmas night, Carolus's mother refused to sleep. She begged his father to run. She scratched his arms. Told him he was a coward. She said many things Carolus couldn't remember well because he was little and it was very late.

"Tell the boy not to go into the music business," his father said. He stayed fixed at that window as if looking away might shatter it.

His mother grew livid. She grabbed at his father's crotch and bit his thighs, an evident desperation he'd never again witnessed. His father wouldn't move and she fell flat at his ankles, kissing them.

"You're a no-good bastard," she said, getting up.

"Go to bed, will you?"

His father's voice always calmed Carolus, and he fell asleep on the stairs listening to his mother sniffle.

Carolus woke to what seemed like a panther eating his father's liver. It wasn't the screaming that woke him; it was the gnawing, yellowed teeth grinding on one another, crooked and blunt. The Yule Cat had torn through his father's throat and was eating him inside out. Carolus walked over. It was not the irreparable horror that first struck him. He admired the cat's long, fishing-wire whiskers. Dried blood matted its hair. It smelled like old newspaper.

Carolus extended his hand as food, as punishment. He used his left and felt guilty for this. The cat sniffed his wrist for a little while and then carefully licked Carolus's fingernails. He'd been eating sugar cookies. Carolus placed his palm on the Yule Cat's head and stroked it. He looked at his father's corpse and pitied it as he felt a hardness grow inside him that would never dissipate. Rage bubbled in his throat; he tasted bile, but he did not move. He stayed still as if it were all a game, as if flinching would keep his father dead. He stayed like that for hours; his only movement—stroking the cat. He could not bring himself to hate the instrument. He wondered if his mother would beat him.

Eventually, Carolus opened the door, and the cat left. The room smelled like blood and urine, and he wanted to let the air come in. He became smaller in the cold doorway. He shut the door and covered his father's body with a blanket that his mother used for reading. And he sat with his father's corpse for a while before falling asleep on the stairs again.

He slept all night with the scent of blood in his nostrils and dreamt of nothing.

* * *

Carolus knocked on Cass's hotel room door.

She opened up, yawning, "Hey."

A little light peeked through the sides of the curtains. He walked in.

"Do you know which room Bjorn's in?" she asked. "I want to talk to him." Her breath smelled stale.

"He left, Cass. I think you should go back, too. It's not safe."

"It's Christmas," she said, limply.

"Happy Christmas." He hugged her tightly.

"You're soaking wet."

"I took a walk."

"Why wouldn't he tell me he went back? Why would he tell *you*?"

"He didn't. I found this note on your door." He handed her a note he'd typed up and printed on the lobby computer. The signature wasn't perfect, but it was adequate. He remembered it from old birthday cards that Cass had made her husband sign.

> *Dear Cass,*
>
> *This trip has made me realize I have to be on my own right now. I know you're unhappy and you have a right to be. I'm a huge piece of shit. I'm going to leave you all my things and the cattle dog because I love you and he is my most prized posses-sion. Please forget about me. I doubt I'll ever return to Iceland.*
>
> *With great love and regret,*
> *Bjorn*
>
> *P.S. Feed him Alpo because the other brands make him gassy.*

"What a coward. Leaving me on Christmas. With a shitty little letter."

Carolus felt confident that his letter was sufficiently absurd and therefore authentic to Bjorn. "I'm so sorry. I figured you wouldn't want to stay around here, so I booked a ticket. It leaves this afternoon." Actu-ally, he'd had Samsa pull some strings at the airline with an old Air Force buddy of his.

"Goddamn it, Carolus. Nobody told you to do that."

"I'll take care of you when I get home. I'll be back tomorrow." He knew he was the only one who could look after his sister now. He hoped that maybe he could bring Delia back with him too. He hoped nothing else would go wrong now that Bjorn was out of the way.

"I'll take care of myself." Cass turned away from Carolus, unable to meet his gaze. "And what about your new girl? Where'd she run off to in the middle of the night?"

"I didn't know she had."

"Well, she's not here. Why don't you find a good Icelandic girl? Someone I don't have to hide my passport around."

He sighed and thought about it for a moment. "Every girl I've ever been with takes a piece of my life." Carolus reached in his pocket where a small reserve of rainwater had built. "If you put them all together, you see me entirely."

"You're using them."

"I carry theirs, too. It's just too much responsibility for one person." The turtle wiggled its star-shaped feet in the air like wings. "What if I fell deeply in love, inconsolably in love, with the first girl I'd ever slept with?"

"You still think about her? You're inconsolable every time."

"What if she died or we had to separate all these years later? How could I ever expect anyone else to know me like that? How could she? We'd be broken to anyone else."

"You're talking about Mom."

"I've left memories scattered all over Iceland."

"I don't think it's memories you've been scattering around." Cass ran her fingernails over her suitcase.

"You're not taking me seriously."

"You're not a serious man, Carolus. No one knows you. Not me, not your first or your last. But you took care of me when you had to, and I love you for that. I'm going home now. I'll see you there?"

He placed a cigarette to his mouth. The turtle gazed at him, its head barely protruding from its shell. Carolus struck a match. He held the matchbook to the window light. It read "Prikid." He nodded to Cass as she zipped up her bag.

"Your girl left this on her pillow," Cass said, tossing him a tiny poseable Jesus figurine before leaving.

* * *

Mornings in Istanbul felt dense, as if the Bosphorus had been dumped over the city. Everyone seemed short-tempered, and very few wore suits or ties to indicate they were busy with professional matters. Carolus stopped and listened for Morning Prayer. The streets had iced over, and cars drove horizontally over the pavement, bumping curbs and posts as they headed toward their destinations.

Carolus walked toward Old Town to meet with Mr. Delicious. In his briefcase: a pistol, a wig, a fake passport, and a change of clothes. On this trip, he was supposed to be Jesús Laird, a Spanish businessman, which, considering everything, was pretty ironic. He didn't feel like Jesús or a Boston, though. He felt too much like Carolus.

He waited outside Mr. Delicious' shop wearing his charcoal blazer, the collar turned up over his neck. He wore leather gloves and blue jeans because it seemed more casual. The night before, once he'd gotten back from the bridge, he watched Delia and Cass in bed, unable to sleep himself. They fell asleep with their backs against one another. In the darkness, he saw their bodies outlined by moonlight and nervous perspiration.

Carolus often lay awake. He imagined the devious and obscure sexualities of Delia's youth. He imagined Astrid's muscular thighs against Delia's lips. The darkness made them closer, and he could hear Cass's heavy breathing on the other side of the bed. He wondered who'd fucked Cass before Bjorn and if she'd ever dreamt about their father. He was suddenly overwhelmed by the sheer girth of the things he'd never know. He recalled Aschel's face, fragmented by alcoholic bliss. The air tasted like copper.

* * *

Mr. Delicious arrived a little earlier than he'd expected, and they walked toward the palace, past houses of prayer and smoke. Mr. Delicious explained that his wife was ill and he was going to have to cut the tour short to check on her because, otherwise, nobody would. Carolus found this moving. For a moment, he considered what mercy would feel like.

"You ever cheat on her?" Carolus asked. He wanted him to say "yes" very badly. He wanted to dislike this man, to question his deliciousness. It had never seemed to matter as much before. He felt a softness in himself that could threaten everything.

Mr. Delicious peered down at his brown loafers as they hiked uphill. His movements seemed very deliberate, as if he was trying not to take any steps in the wrong direction. "I did this, yes."

Carolus felt relief wash over him, though the honesty threw him. "Most people would hesitate to admit that."

"I do not find it necessary to lie to a stranger. I lie to those close to me, Mr. Boston."

Carolus swung his briefcase back and forth with his right hand as he walked. "To protect them?"

The man never answered. As they approached the palace, which lay on the top of a steep hill, a film of dry light surrounded Topkapi, and frost from the night before tumbled off its minarets. Carolus hadn't anticipated the metal detectors he now spotted in the distance. Flop sweat collected on his back and nose.

"I have to piss," he said.

Mr. Delicious breathed heavily, lowered his gaze over the chopped cobblestones and then straight up the narrow hill. "It is only some few minutes."

"My prostate is the size of a tropical gourd," Carolus lied.

"That is unfortunate for a man of your small age."

The road pointed upward with small stone rivulets, leading into banks of trees and tombstones where traitors and pear thieves had been buried. Mr. Delicious explained these details to Carolus as they walked.

"Go over there," he said. Mr. Delicious pointed toward a patch of hyacinths away from the path. "I will look out." He turned his back to Carolus and watched for guards. Carolus approached the hyacinths and a worn, unheralded grave in the ground, unzipped his jeans, and dropped his briefcase into the brush. He pissed a little for effect, reading the English plaque next to the gravestone:

Here was Amir, King of his people for one day and six hours and never again.

Carolus zipped up. "Thanks," he said earnestly, and they resumed their climb. He hoped that Mr. Delicious would be too distracted to notice he'd left his briefcase.

Muted by bare, white trees, Topkapi's entrance stood ancient and medieval with a stone gate flanked by wooden spires. Carolus envisioned similar betrayals within its walls—men lying next to Turkish Guinevere.

At the entrance, the security guard wanded Carolus and Mr. Delicious. The former's mind wandered far away to Tjörnin Pond and how rarely he'd dipped his small body into its murky waters. He remembered leaving his arm in as long as he could one November until he couldn't feel it anymore. When he got home, he found his mother sick. He put his purplish wrist on her warm forehead.

"That feels good," she said, her eyes closed and fluttering to the pastel flashes of *Lazytown* on TV. It was an Icelandic children's program where only two of the characters were real and the man had a cartoonish mustache like Errol Flynn but much longer. Carolus always wondered why she liked it.

"It hurts," Carolus said, twisting his arm over her dry lips and cheeks like a rolling pin.

"Leave it," she said.

His arm tingled warm even though the room was cold. He wished Cass were home because she'd know what to do.

* * *

The security guard pushed Carolus through the metal detector and into the palace. Inside, Mr. Delicious walked a path set apart from the other tourists, one that led to a white building with multicolored marble columns. This, he said, was the harem.

"You are familiar with such structures, yes?"

Carolus thought back to a time when he felt consumed by sexuality. When he'd confess to masturbation and fantasizing about his uncle's new wife. She'd reminded him of Ingrid Bergman, and he would wrap a tube sock around his member and stuff it under his textbooks afterward. He recalled endless prayers for respite—prayers like dandelion seed floating toward the Reykjavik moon. In the winters, when there was such little light, the moon became a constant fixture in his predatory inventions. He dreamt of rooms wallpapered in women, chained to sharp crescents, howling. He couldn't express his deviance properly to the pastor, so he figured it best to carve these images in the snow so that they might disappear into the salt and black rock. It was only the Lads, years later, who would understand.

Each room in the harem reeked of holy copulation. The walls ornately depicted faded floral patterns where stamen penetrated tree trunks and beehives. Dark mannequins portrayed what a sultan might have looked like surrounded by extremely unsexual women shrouded in black and with doll eyes plucked from children's toys.

Past the harem was another section of small palatial rooms. These contained artifacts of the holy ancient world of relics. Walking side by side with Mr. Delicious, Carolus searched for anything he could use as a weapon. There were points, though, when he forgot his mission for a moment and admired the footprint of Mohammed, the rod of Moses, the armor of great Turkish princes, heretical shrouds, sheik's crowns, and curved and serrated yatagans.

A guard wandered back and forth outside the open door, a cigarette in his mouth, his hands bothered slightly by the cold. As the call to prayer sounded, Carolus suffered the words in his bones. He wondered if saving Mr. Delicious' life would mean something.

A singer in white prayer garb chanted into a microphone. It reminded Carolus of warm nights in the Reykjavik Theatre basement, where sometimes luscious Svana would be learning her lines for the Christmas pageant. He'd watch her, averting his adolescent eyes any time she'd look up.

Mr. Delicious stopped by the rod of Moses for a closer look. Carolus stood straight to his right so that their coats touched. The other tourists passed through, and now only the prayer chanter remained in the next room. Mr. Delicious heightened his voice so that it was impossible to hear beyond a meter or two.

"Does this mean something to you?" he asked.

Carolus placed his hand on the glass. There was no guard present to stop him. It wasn't as thick as he suspected. The rod was only a thin piece of whittled Sycamore, unadorned, about three meters long.

"Anything that parts the Red Sea impresses me a little," Carolus said.

"God parted the sea."

"Men always impressed me more. We have more to overcome than Gods."

Mr. Delicious leaned down and breathed on the glass, his breath revealing hundreds of oily fingerprints. "We are coarse in ways you cannot dream. I am coarse," he said.

"Something to confess, Mr. Delicious?"

He placed his hand over Carolus's on the shallow glass above the rod.

"I am maybe not so delicious as I have led everyone to think."

His hard, dry skin pressed on Carolus, who could feel the stiff wrinkles that had begun to form in his fingertips. He was suddenly older, Carolus realized.

"Have you ever imagined death upon yourself as a quiet serpent?" Mr. Delicious tightened his grip on Carolus.

Carolus had often dreamt up phrases that could explain death precisely as he felt it. "I imagine the uncoupling of providence," he said finally. It was a line he'd used in one of his journals.

"I'd not imagined you as a romantic."

At the height of the sung prayer, Carolus swung his free arm with all his force in a windmill and crashed down on the display, slashing both of their hands. Blood spread over the glass. Mr. Delicious grabbed a shard and lurched at Carolus's eyes. Carolus twisted away as the shard narrowly missed his throat. He was afraid to die. He felt it in his loins. He grabbed the rod of Moses, lifted it above his head, and hit Mr. Delicious twice in the temple. The chanter, unaware, continued in the adjoining room as Carolus struck the man's head repeatedly until his skull collapsed into the tile.

He dropped the rod and peeked out to where the guard stood; he hadn't heard. The guard leaned against the villa wall and poked out his tongue to taste the fresh snowfall.

Carolus covered his bloodied fingers and walked past the guard toward the exit. Behind him, a man screamed. He exited Topkapi and felt very quiet inside himself. He didn't feel remorseful or condemned as he thought he might have on the Lord's Day. Carolus picked up his briefcase and crossed back over the bridge. He felt very alone and thought of an old girlfriend who loved him and the cheap promises he now hardly recalled. He imagined buying pickled tomatoes with Delia.

CHAPTER 25

Carolus feared his work had been sloppy. He'd enacted violence with the holiest of artifacts. And perhaps most dangerously of all, he'd committed murder inside the palace walls and insulted Turkishness—a high crime.

As far as forensics are concerned, however, he'd been as clean as ever, aside from the blood. He wasn't on anyone's file. He figured it would be a day or two before the Turks matched anything to the information Bjorn had given them, though they might have his photo. It would be prudent to head home to Cass; Istanbul was closing in on him, but he couldn't go back without finding Delia.

Before heading back, he stopped at a small café and ordered a carafe of Raki. He sat by the window, watching passersby struggle with their long coats and fight against the snowfall. The anisette flavor cooled his throat, but the burn brought back memories of a traditional Icelandic wedding he'd attended once.

* * *

It was very lavish. At the reception, he sat at the high table along with the bride, groom, best man, and the hired toastmaster, whose job it was to get everyone drunk.

In truly traditional weddings such as that one, the bridesmaids take the bride back to her bed at the end of the reception to undress her completely except for her headdress—a wicker tiara streaming with powder blue ribbons passed down through generations. There, naked and brimming with Brennevin-emboldened sexuality, she waits for her newly appointed husband to join her. As he removes the headdress, the priest blesses them one last time, drinks from their bridal cups, and seals the marriage.

Carolus recalled the research he conducted—learning the prayers and the gesticulations of a priest, paying off the clergymen. He was careful only to give the atropine to the man and a sedative to the woman, but as the groom's capillaries burst and the life spewed out of him, the man called out to God to save him.

Carolus loved using atropine because it felt more sensual than other poisons. Belladonna they called it—only a few berries from the nightshade bush. How theatrical, he thought.

"Can't you help me?" the groom begged.

Carolus straightened his purple robes over his flat body. He was younger then, more fit. "It was a beautiful ceremony," he said. "I ate too much, I think. You ever feel like that?"

The man turned his flushed, sweaty head to his wife. He began to wheeze.

"I won't hurt her," Carolus assured him, though he fought a sickeningly strong impulse to pull the covers back from the naked bride, now nearly unconscious below him. But he had more respect for the sanctity of marriage. He wished he were the groom dying next to her warm, soft body.

* * *

Carolus didn't mind being hunted. It seemed like a nice change of pace. He was still haunted by regrets of a passive youth. He remembered Otta, seventeen, in her orange dress listening to her Walkman before they went to see a movie. He recalled how long her legs were, how she smiled when she saw him. The whole movie she looked over and smiled. He did too, but he never acted. They talked afterward over stew. When they said goodbye, he kissed her on the cheek and never saw her again. That was regret. It disgusted him that he was once that boy. And that's why he was being hunted now. You hunt what you fear, he thought.

He imagined himself and Delia fucking. He wished he could see the passenger and the driver again. He thought of all the fledgling relationships he'd killed, both literally and figuratively. But there was something romantic about being the cause of one's own misery.

CHAPTER 26

December 26
Feast Day of the Pagan God Jul

Sol Invictus—the "unconquerable sun." On the twelfth night, the Christmas decorations came down, and Carolus's mother cooked a small family pheasant. Carolus knew this night would herald many long, dark evenings in Iceland. His mother would tell stories of saints and pagan gods dancing in Reykjavik bonfires. Although they surely never existed together, the tales were entertaining and the night always flickered past twelve and his bedtime.

Cass would wear her blue cotton nightgown because she'd exhausted her fine clothes during the many days of Christmas and since it was only immediate family (no uncles). Carolus often thought about his uncles as oafish fiends who preyed on older women only because the young ones laughed at them. The feast of Jul was also the night that began the departure of the Yule Lads and the countdown to January 6, on which the elves would move from rock to rock, celebrating with carefully chosen peasants worthy of their ancient tongue.

Carolus felt very blessed to have spoken once with one of the elves at length about music and number two pencils. This was one of their favorite subjects, he found. It was sad to see them go. Often, Christmas was their only human interaction all year. Lads were known as recluses and rarely, if ever, threw holiday galas. Cass never seemed to mind when they left. She'd be occupied with a boy or teasing several boys—the many weightlifting hambones who frequented the gym or rowed through the icy rivers.

* * *

The cops in their neat little uniforms formed fascistic lines in the streets of Istanbul like synchronized swimmers. As evening came on and the snow fell harder, they clicked on periwinkle flashlights and blew whistles to find each other, holding hands to stay erect against the deep winds.

From above it must have resembled windmill spokes—the snow obscuring their beams so each flake illuminated brilliant before it burned at their hands. As a wave started down his block, Carolus searched for a place to hide. He ducked into a red-awninged travel agency.

He knew he had to leave. Something was keeping him here, even beyond Delia. A feeling of incompletion. The only things left for him in Istanbul were prison and death. Providence had led him here, and yet he'd lost Delia again. He prayed she was safe. She was free now, after all, though the thought of it made him cringe.

"You like to take the cruise?" a Turkish man holding a Starbucks cup asked. He looked like Danny DeVito.

"No, no more cruises," Carolus said.

"Why be in the weather when you could go to Greece? You take a boat. You are there. End of story." He put down his steaming coffee and placed his hand on Carolus's shoulder. He looked outside at the snow now falling harder. "You go somewhere warmer, maybe. You come back to cruise with the ladies; I know you like this." He winked awkwardly at Carolus, fingering the mug handle.

Carolus knew he wasn't safe there at the moment, so as soon as the cops swept past, he made his way to the door.

"You wait," the agent said.

Carolus wondered if his gun showed through his blazer. He froze near the doorway. He wondered how many lives were worth his own.

"You take this. You seem like a man of means." The agent handed him his card. "If you need. I am filled with discretion."

Carolus nodded. A lucky break. Maybe he'd found a way out of Turkey. But for the time being, he had to lay low until night came on completely. Outside, he noticed a police car parked in front and quickly skulked away. He checked the business card:

Albedo Turizm:
Tulin Far, World Agent

Walking north, Carolus passed a McDonald's and a man hanging off a signpost trying to sell shoes. He also had belts, but they were of inferior quality. There wasn't much room on the sidewalks because of the snow, so he lowered his head to the wind and crossed into the street. Behind him, lights flashed and he decided to duck into an alleyway filled with marmalade cats and goat hair scarves. He became increasingly mired in the long alleyway with closed storefronts lining either side. The only other person in the alley was an old woman wearing a kerchief on her head. She walked toward him. Her legs were thick and stretched the cheap thread of her brown skirt. She was oddly flat-chested for an old Turkish lady. As he got closer, she came toward him—and then, swooping out of the shadows, her fist met his nose and knocked him straight back.

He lay on the floor like the snow angels he'd violated many years before, legs spread apart, and he checked his bloody nose. "That's a real hook you've got, you old bitch."

"You are the bitch in this scenario here," a familiar voice said.

"Astrid?" He never thought he'd hear such broken English again. But what was she doing here and why was she dressed as an old woman? Carolus checked around the alley. The storm rendered it hollow and disconnected from the rest of the city. Ice drifted in like fog and Astrid's paisley dress fluttered.

"I am not unreasonable. You know this." She got down, pressing her knee to Carolus's belly and held down his shoulders. "I tried to know you. I wanted to have convincing that I should not end your existence."

"My existence?"

"Your living situation. Your existence. No?"

Carolus reached down into his pocket, pulled out cigarettes, and placed one in his mouth, stretching the free range Astrid allowed him. "Light?"

"Fuck you." Astrid banged Carolus's head against the pavement, dazing him. He noticed a long, infected cut, a few days old, across Astrid's cheek.

"Where'd you get that scar?" Carolus knew he had to stall, stay calm. He wasn't yet sure what Astrid's true intentions were. Carolus's head bled slightly through his hair.

Astrid licked the side of her mouth where the cut began and ran up to her sideburn. It must have been from Delia the night at the factory, Carolus suddenly realized—those long mint nails.

"It is a sin to turn one's wife against her. You make her ugly."

Carolus bit down on the cigarette. "I'm sorry about Delia. I should never have come in between you. It's—there was something I couldn't be without."

"You think because you can talk that it saves you, that God does not see what you bring on this world. I am your reckoning." Astrid swung her head down, biting at Carolus, tearing a piece of flesh from his neck. Carolus sprung up and flung Astrid against a rack of rabbit skins, sending her crashing through the wood.

Carolus covered the gash in his neck. "I'm in the middle of something, Astrid. If you leave, I'll just forget it."

Astrid growled like a wolf, blood streaming down her chin. She pulled out a .60 caliber she'd been hiding under her skirt. She sprang like a wolf leaping off its hind legs, careening back into Carolus. As the gun rose to Carolus's head, he didn't reach for his silenced pistol. Calm overtook him. He thought back to when he was a boy. When his father was still in charge.

* * *

For a short time, when his father was doing well, they hired a Polish cleaning lady to help around the house on Tuesdays. Carolus was only eight, but he remembered sneaking behind the oak banister on the first landing and watching her change out of her blue scrubs. The enormity of her breasts hidden neatly behind her thick, white bra gave Carolus purpose. He could only guess at their texture and weight—similar perhaps to holding a balled-up cat, even in so much as they might squirm out of his hands at the slightest touch.

It was unique voyeurism because it was innocent and because he always felt like she knew. He found that same acquiescence in Delia all these years later. It was irresistible. To change right out in the living room where she knew he could watch.

After viewing the woman, Carolus would carefully slip upstairs and take three small papaya pills from his mother's medicine cabinet. They tasted sweet, and his mother said to have them when his stomach felt funny.

Carolus couldn't remember the maid's name now or her face, which he assumed, however blurred in his memory, would no longer appear beautiful to him.

* * *

Astrid held the gun at his neck. She'd take the shot. He knew that now. Carolus considered that he might die never having ended his journey, never recovering Delia. He imagined her scolding him for not bringing home yogurt and how he would squeeze her side as she passed him in their house. She'd be wearing blue and smell of citrus. His mother had told him many years ago that Achilles, when confronted in the underworld, said he'd have given up all his battle glory to live as a farmer. Maybe she was trying to warn him. The only sounds Carolus heard now were the occasional passing vehicle and the soft sift of the sky descending over Istanbul.

Astrid's hands shook from the weight of her barrel-heavy hand cannon. Sweat dripped into her eyes, even in the cold. Carolus's hands remained steady. He braced himself as the pistol reached his temple.

Abruptly, a flutter came from within Carolus's chest. Three black gnats rose from his body. He couldn't believe they'd followed him all this way and he felt dirty, as if they bred within him. As if by some divine compass, they flew straight into Astrid's eyes, and she jerked back. The gun discharged. The bang echoed off the walls of the cobblestone alleyway. Blood streamed from Carolus's ear. His head rang. The bullet strayed right.

Carolus and Astrid jammed their backs against the alley walls, up against yak belts and muslin dresses. Carolus grabbed for his silenced Ruger and trained it on Astrid.

"You must have a devil's deal." Astrid shook her head in disbelief, wiping her eyes with her sleeve. "Who is it do you think I am? This bored traveler just happening to hit your head with a football trophy?" The words came out muffled to Carolus, his ears ringing. He watched Astrid's lips. "You thought I was someone else."

Carolus felt foolish for believing her. His ear throbbed and bled, but pain was something he could deal with. He checked his pocket for the turtle with his bloody hand and felt over its shell, perfectly intact.

"Do you remember the name Tomas Grumson?" Astrid asked.

It was the name on the trophy; but what did it mean? "I'm ready for the explanation." Blood dribbled down his neck.

"Maybe you remember Sten Grumson. You suffocated this man using a plant."

"It was a Ficus."

"So you do remember this." Astrid licked her dry lips.

"You're saying he wasn't dead?"

"He was extremely dead. You choked him with this Ficus, then you shot him. No, he had a sister, Mr. Carolus. That sister is me. Your client—that was my friend, Carlos. Tomas is Sten's son. My nephew. Did you know he had a son?"

"No. I don't look into those things. It's a rabbit hole."

"You are the rabbit hole, Mr. Carolus. I desired to watch you. Talk with you. I wanted understanding of what a monster is."

Could it all be true? Carolus paused. "And Mr. Delicious?"

"You were never supposed to get to him. Just a candy man with reduced luck. You feel no remorse. But he will have died for good causes. No waste."

"Why didn't you kill me on the train?"

The two combatants breathed in the biting air—Carolus bleeding, Astrid adjusting her bra through the dress. Each with a finger on a trigger.

"It was of importance to me that you suffer in your mind. I wanted to know this sick fuck who kills good, pacific men. The Arab I hired to gain your trust. I should have disposed of him long before. He thought he was doing favors for me. I do not kill with indiscrimination like you. I am no animal." She rubbed her thumb along the butt of her gun. She licked her wet lips.

"Of course, he had no comprehension I would Jesus him. Delia was supposed to drug you in Prague; I even have premium torturer lined up. He takes weeks to book. She refused. You are impressionable to young women, even mine. Fucked my own wife, so things became even more personal. That should not have been. I was weakened then. And what do you consider more personal than civilizing a discussion before death? I never told the policemen about you. Why would I give them this pleasure?" She tilted her head and puffed out her chest.

"Where's Delia?" Carolus kept aim on Astrid, blood leaking into the snow. With his free hand, he grabbed a scarf from one of the racks behind him and wrapped it loosely around his head.

The storm picked up, and it was hard to see in front of them. Behind them, Carolus caught the faint blur of blue police lights. They must have heard the shot. Even if they weren't after him before, he thought, they might be for Mr. Delicious. The man was a column of the community.

A wave of fatigue washed over Astrid, and he widened his eyes. "You think I know of her location. I told you this; you ruined her to me."

"I like your dress."

"It is interesting what some people are amused by," Astrid said. "It worked since I received the first blow to you." Her body slumped down, and he seemed very small in the vastness of the drift.

"Drink?"

"You do not seem like a type of spontaneousness. Is this the right word? Spontaneousness?"

"Just about," Carolus said.

"It is a fine word. But yes, you feel like you plan, and the man without the plan is always the more dangerous."

Watching one another very carefully, they tucked their guns and began to walk side by side. A criminal trust grew momentarily between them, and they made an unspoken agreement to not kill one another until they reached the café. The police lights faded, obscured in white. Nearby, Hotel Romance seemed to have an operating bar with a keep. Red barbell-shaped lamps hung from the low ceiling, and the room smelled of tart apples—probably from the hookah. At the bar, several men watched a football match. Their mustaches appeared fantastic to Carolus. He and Astrid sat down at a square table catty-cornered from the bar.

"Whisky," Carolus growled to the bartender, showing the size of the bottle he wanted with his hands. Windows surrounded them, so Carolus knew he could smash one if he needed to make a quick exit.

The keep brought over a sizeable bottle of Jameson and two tumblers. As he placed the bottle, he seemed taken aback Carolus's state: bloodied, a scarf around his head and Astrid's shabby appearance. The last thing he needed was for the bartender to call the cops. But then, as if he'd seen it all before, he shrugged and tended to another table.

"So why not shoot me straight off? Why the theatrics?" Carolus asked.

He poured two shots of whisky and handed one to Astrid. They clinked glasses and drank down the sting.

"I live this life as if every experience was a mango. I love mangos and suck them dry when I have them."

Carolus coughed a little, which he was not accustomed to. The drink was warm and tough. He poured himself and Astrid another shot. Their noses ran from the cold, yellow and red, Carolus wobbled from the loss of blood. He sweated under the scarf, his ear pulsing. His gun lay under a napkin on his lap. He was unsure where Astrid kept hers. They each made sure to show both gloved hands on the table.

"I've been thinking about quitting," Carolus said, and maybe this was true. It didn't feel good anymore. He had no one except for Cass, and now he'd widowed her on a hunch. God—it all just hit him. Bjorn was completely innocent. He killed him in cold blood like one of those pigs squealing from the hook.

"It's too late to quit, friend," Astrid said.

"What would you say to walking away from this? Your brother—he's gone. It was someone else who wanted him dead."

"This is something you can say to me with a narrow face?"

Carolus figured she meant straight face.

"It is as if you have committed no crime," Astrid continued. "You are told to do so, so you do. What if I pay you one million euros to end your miserable life? You do this for me?"

"We're all just trying to survive," Carolus said, earnest. It was a case he'd often thought of and wrote about in his failed book attempts. "Take a beetle, for instance. He develops a hard shell. You crush him with your finger and you could swear you feel him crack under your nail." He mashed his thumb into the pine table. "But when you lift your thumb, he's writhing, half-dead, trying to squirm away. Now what kind of life will that beetle live? For how much longer? It would be easier to die, to have given in to the weight of your thumb. But that's only because we see its life as insignificant, and we crush it because it gets into our line of sight. All it wants is to live. If you'd seen what I've seen, you'd realize that we're exactly the same in our final instants. You claw for every second you have left on this earth, and you go out screaming because if you can scream, you exist."

"Are you saying my brother screamed like a beetle before his death?"

Carolus tried to remember the specifics of Sten Grumson's passing, but it would only have upset Astrid further. He could see she had reached a dark place. "You're taking the story all wrong. It was about me. I'm the beetle." He thought about Cass and how selfish he'd been. She'd have no one now if he were gone.

"There is a word I am very proud to learn. Impasse. This is impasse," Astrid said.

Carolus called over the bartender and handed him the turtle, which peeked around a little before switching hands. "Put him in water. He likes that." He handed him the eye drops, too, and 200 lira. Astrid understood what this meant as well. She stared intently into Carolus as if she'd found weakness.

For a moment, the only sounds in the bar were of patrons chewing almonds and the TV emitting the tinny sound of football chants. Without ceremony, Astrid dropped her hands under the table and came up firing. The blasts shook the bar and sent liquor and glass flying everywhere. Carolus flipped the table for cover. The drinkers scattered and screamed. None of the shots had landed. Carolus picked up the base of the table and blindly rammed forward behind it as bullets shattered wood around him, splintering into his cheeks. He crashed into Astrid, sending him back against the wall.

Carolus's scarf flew off and his ear dripped as he searched for his gun in the debris. Astrid moaned behind the table, so Carolus jumped over and smashed her across the face, grabbed her weapon. They struggled to point it at one another. Carolus forced the magnum toward Astrid's mouth until it clicked against her gritting teeth—metal against enamel. Carolus searched Astrid's eyes; there were tears. Carolus remembered his mother, preserved in youth, heating stew for him, Cass, and their father. He felt full. Sated on memory. As he pulled the trigger, he felt his own death as the shell of Astrid's skull sprayed across the room and down her oversized paisley dress.

Carolus took a moment before he could move, wiped some of the excess blood from his eyes and nose, breathing heavy. He tucked the gun into his pants and walked languidly to the bar. The bartender recoiled under the rum section. "I'll be needing that turtle now," Carolus said.

CHAPTER 27

December 27

Carolus woke up staring into the turtle's desolate eyes. It waded in a pool of inky blood by his pillow, rotating its flippers in semi-circles. He recognized his surroundings. It was the hotel. He must have gotten himself back, although he didn't remember how. The knocks to the head and the loss of blood put him out pretty good, he figured. It was amazing that no one followed him.

His neck and forehead pounded. The previous evening flooded back to him. He hadn't found Delia. He searched for a clean shirt and showered, dried blood twisting down the drain like chocolate syrup. When he got out, he wrapped his ear in gauze from his suitcase, dressed in unsullied slacks and a gray sweater, and left everything else under the bed with the body. The body stunk like rotting eggs, and it reminded Carolus of Iceland. Of the hot springs, his daily showers, and the smell of boiling ham.

Before he left, Carolus hung a "Do Not Disturb" sign on the door, didn't check out. He left the bodies for Bedrich. At the front desk, he left an envelope filled with cash and a note to the bellhop who'd accommodated him. He figured he'd already fucked up enough for one job. He thought of his mother asking him to clean out the ashtrays all over the house. They always seemed to be full, even the one in the bathroom. He'd pick them out one by one, made the job painstaking, and infuriated her in the distances of the house. Each cigarette left a lipstick fingerprint, and he liked to count the days between each red-coated cigarette because his mother wore makeup according to her mood. Often, the ashtrays filled up with brown.

The sun began to rise ominously over the ice-driven city. He left the motel with a sick feeling that he would never see Delia again and an even more disturbing inkling that he'd overstayed his welcome.

Though still covered in a thick white blanket, Istanbul seemed to have revived itself, bustling and steaming as it had in the days before Christmas. Carolus resigned himself to wandering. The city felt no less magical than when he'd arrived, but its alleys and mazes confused him. He found himself driven deeper and deeper into the curves of the sprawl, guided only by the water and mosque spires leading him toward Asia.

He checked every melon shop and ratchet store along the way—unable to read the signs, searching. It was all futile, he knew. Each shop took some breath out of him, and although he'd been walking for hours, the arches of his feet were in pins. As a child he'd been told he had flat feet.

One business after another, he inquired after Delia. Sometimes store owners would greet him, sit him down for apple tea and gum, and sometimes they'd ignore him. Maybe because of his face and bandages.

And then, opening a door to a yellow room cluttered with cubicles, as mundanely as running into an old babysitter or tailor, he saw Aschel. She sat behind a metal desk, slouched, talking into a Motorola headset. As he walked toward her, her eyes said that she recognized him. She wore a knee-length gray skirt and a green cardigan. He stood a few feet away from her. She covered her mouthpiece but did not stand. It was some kind of Turkish phone service. No one seemed to notice him. Why should they, Carolus thought, their situation wasn't all that unusual—boy creates girl, girl creates man, girl works in telemarketing. She parted her lips but remained silent.

She was unmistakably real. The headset microphone hovered in front of her lips, which he now saw were blistered from the cold. Carolus wanted to tell her he would die with her, that he could pounce on her, beg for her, that no one could ever fail him more. Instead, he walked out of the little travel storefront. Aschel was too real. Maybe no one would ever compare to Delia. He had one last place to look for her before she was lost forever.

His briefcase in hand, he hailed a red cab, which skidded to a stop in front of him.

"Where are you going, my friend?" the cabbie asked.

Carolus straightened his palm and raised it up on a diagonal until his fingertips hit the roof.

"Heading home?"

"Let me ask you something," Carolus sighed as the driver pulled out, "Do I seem delicious to you?" Carolus caught a glimpse of himself in the rearview mirror. He looked spent, beaten.

At the next stop sign, the driver looked back. Carolus hadn't slept, fresh blood on his neck, torn coat, overgrown beard.

"You are the most delicious customer I have today."

Carolus clutched his case in his lap. "That actually means a lot."

* * *

The travel agent Carolus had met the day before arranged for him to stow away to Prague in a shipment of lentils. The boy had friends at the airport, he said. Carolus paid him exorbitantly through wire transfer. He exited as part of the flight crew and took off toward the Poseable Religious Emporium, where he hoped he'd find Delia.

On the plane, lying next to crates of lentils, Carolus felt humbled. His pride and vengeance had brought him nothing, and he surely awaited punishment in the next. He felt alone as he and the turtle closed their eyes. He drifted in and out of a sweaty sleep while the haze of small, tortured dreams overtook him.

When he arrived in Prague, he paid homage to Kafka's house, which was small and indistinguishable in the dense snowfall. Afterward, he wandered the city in search of the emporium. By the time he stumbled upon it, it was already night. The front doors weren't locked, so he wandered in. A few of the ceiling lamps cast yellow beams through a thin film of dust wafting throughout the factory. "Delia?"

From the farthest corner, he saw her. She emerged timidly, unsure who was calling. She wore a blue dress and had tied her hair back into a ponytail. He hardly noticed her appearance at all when he saw her. He only felt her presence, and it was warm. He wondered if he had the right to hold someone so beautiful.

"Where is Astrid?" she asked flatly.

The question jarred him. Carolus searched the factory as he reflected on the finality of his journey. She'd cleaned up a little and the electricity was on. Maybe she was trying to open up shop again, he thought.

"I killed her."

Delia brought her hand to her mouth, her mint nails against her cheek. Sad, a little, but not angry. She came closer, nodding to Carolus as if she understood. She knew what he was in that moment—that things had to end this way because death had become his language and religion. Carolus could see guilt creep into her eyes since, in a way, she was relieved.

"I have to plan for the funeral," she said. "Her mother will blame me."

"I'm sure that's not true."

"You have not met her mother. She is like an angry badger."

"I'm sorry," Carolus said, realizing that he felt remorse, too. He felt it for her. And for Bjorn who'd committed no crime other than marrying into his family and perhaps carrying the cattle dog on his chest.

Delia walked over behind her desk and pulled out a wrapped gift—a box the size of a sun hat, wrapped in metallic sea green paper and tied with a red bow. "I was hoping I'd see you again. The contents of it allow you to peer into my soul at exactly this moment. Don't ever open it."

"That hardly seems like a gift. I feel like I should give you something equally mysterious."

She walked closer, handed him the box. "There's no sense in competing." She ran her fingernails along the length of it, letting her hair drape over her shoulder. "Maybe you can visit sometime, if you're living."

He set the turtle on a nearby conveyor belt next to Delia. "He needs to be in water sometimes, and he likes kebab. He's Turkish." He handed her the eye drops. "Twice a day."

"He'll like it here," she cooed, gently rubbing its shell.

The turtle retreated inside.

"His name's Mr. Delicious," Carolus said.

"That's quite a name for a little turtle."

"He's my legacy."

Carolus hopped onto the conveyor and pushed the yellow button next to it. Slowly, with a misting of dust, it began to move and Delia hoisted herself on, her black heels dangling beneath her, an inch off her stockinged heel. Languidly, they slunk through the factory, the turtle between them as if they themselves were being assembled. And Carolus felt a sense of romantic family: something he knew Cass could never provide. Their legs swung like fleshy marionettes as they weaved in and out of boxes and partitions, unsure when they would stop.

That night they made love and, in the morning, Carolus waited for her to wake. His heart beat quickly as he followed her breath and the way her lips moved when she slept. He knew then that he could never have that kind of happiness. He hadn't earned it. He kissed her gently, took the box she'd given him, and left.

* * *

Carolus found himself on a small boat back home. As the vessel approached Iceland, Carolus stood at the hull clutching Delia's gift. He wondered how something so tangible and poorly wrapped could hold a soul.

In the sky, a swirling green light appeared, and Carolus found it very moving. He finally saw the Northern lights—serpentine, ephemeral—and he felt, if not worthy, fortunate. He'd never open the box, he told himself. He'd found something civilized in Delia. Something he didn't destroy. Quickly, the sky bruised gray and only the dull beams beneath the ship echoed in the churning black waters.

Carolus wanted to stay out in the glacial night air until the boat docked. He breathed in the bitter cold, the salt; he tasted insomnia. He didn't know how to sleep anymore. His eyes sagged and his head lolled as the hull rocked against the break. After a while, he noticed a young German woman hugging the railing with her back turned to the sea. He hadn't noticed her step outside. She approached him.

"Do you mind if I smoke?" Her voice did not betray her age. It was steady and thick. It was hard to tell, in the shadows, what her face looked like, except that she was pale because she reflected what little light there was. Her thin body arched against the railing, resembling a cross.

"Go ahead," Carolus said.

"No."

"No?"

"That is, may I borrow one of yours?"

Carolus smiled. It seemed no one could really say what she wanted to anymore. He pulled out two cigarettes, lit one in his mouth and the other with his own, handing it to her.

"Danka—did you see them?" She pointed her thumb to the north.

Carolus took a pull, and the smoke swirled up and off toward land. In the distance, small cities appeared, faint and yellow like eyes in the forest. "I did, actually."

She paused as if considering whether or not to speak. "I am coming here without a lodging." Her hair thrashed wildly behind her. The boat growled softly under them. "Would you happen to have space for me, maybe?"

Carolus leaned over the railing, his cigarette dragging in the misting wind. He thought of how often he dreamt of this, still pinning Delia's present to his chest. "I have someone else I have to see tonight. Her husband's gone 'cause of me."

"I can see how you might have that effect." She tossed her cigarette into the wake and followed the railing back into the boat.

CHAPTER 28

December 31
Gamlárskvöld: New Year's Eve

New Year's was a time for magic, a night when the elves would change houses and the young lit bonfires down the icy coast, dancing like pagans against the cold. Fireworks spider-legged across the morning—bursting, undulating over the Reykjavik skyline.

In the past, Carolus would sit in the crossroads of the highway by the National Park and wait for the elves to sprint by on their way to change rocks for the year. He'd hoped for Elfin gold to bring back to his mother; once, he saw a beautiful elf who'd caught her white robe on some branches. He watched her struggle before he helped and felt guilty that he was so excited by it. They were far better creatures than he.

He remembered twirling in dizzying revolutions into the snow with Cass by the fires, by the cold blue sea. They drank, though they were not yet old enough, and discussed the politics of the Yule Lads, who'd even then begun to lean toward the right. They sang and chanted until the moon turned gold and the sky went green with Christmas.

This year it rained. The government cancelled the bonfires, and Carolus sat at home with Cass, the cattle dog lying across both their laps. It breathed heavily, drowning out the sounds of the old house.

Carolus stared at the clocks and old pictures on the wall and he felt very far away from the crackling, ecstatic celebrations.

"So he's gone then?" Carolus asked, referring to Bjorn.

Cass pulled up her sweater on her sore throat. "Looks like it."

"You remember when Dad ate all the Gorgonzola before everyone got here, and we had to go out on New Year's Eve and find some more?"

Cass coughed. "Not really." She picked up her tea and sipped it.

The mint wafted over them and the dog began sniffing wildly.

"Did you see any of the elves moving today?"

"You're not still going on about those things are you? Yule Lads and all that?"

Carolus turned square to Cass. "Well it's fact. They're fact. I talked to them. I knew them."

She sniffled and patted him on the thigh. "My little brother."

The clock meandered toward twelve.

Just then, something moved outside the house, displacing the sleet for a moment by the window. Carolus removed the cattle dog from his lap and hurried to the window. He cupped his hands around his cheeks and rubbed the window clear. "You see that?"

The cattle dog stood proudly next to him by the sill. He opened the door and without bothering to put on a coat, entered the wet darkness with only the house light to guide him.

"Where are you going? It's cold," Cass said.

He shut the door behind him. Shivering in his brown leather slippers, he stepped out onto the wet earth and searched for what he already knew was there. By the log pile to the left of the porch, he saw two green eyes. He walked toward them, the cattle dog jingling slowly behind him. The eyes continued to brighten, unblinking and holy.

"Are you moving? Is that why you're here?"

The eyes came toward him and, in the darkness, he knelt. Into the dim light slunk the outline of a small brown cat. Water seeped up through his pants, and the cat licked his fingers before it scurried off into the darkness.

Carolus went back inside with the cattle dog.

"Find any g-nomes out there?" Cass asked, having trouble speaking through her stuffed nose.

He sat back down, the cold creeping up into his thighs. The cattle dog stretched over their laps, still trembling and wet. "You shoulda seen it, Cass. You should've been there."

ABOUT THE AUTHOR

Matthew Di Paoli has been nominated for the Pushcart Prize three times. He has won the Wilbur & Niso Smith Adventure Writing Prize, the Prism Review, 2 Elizabeth's, and Momaya Review Short Story Contests. Matthew earned his MFA in Fiction at Columbia University. He has been published in Boulevard, Fjords, Post Road, and Cleaver, among others. He is the author of *Holliday* with Sunbury Press.